# PRIMAL MALE

Books By Sasha White

PURE SEX

THE COP

LUSH

SEXY DEVIL

PRIMAL MALE

Published by Kensington Publishing Corporation

# PRIMAL MALE

## SASHA WHITE

APHRODISIA

KENSINGTON BOOKS

http://www.kensingtonbooks.com

APHRODISIA BOOKS are published by

Kensington Publishing Corp.
850 Third Avenue
New York, NY 10022

All Kensington Titles, Imprints, and Distributed Lines are available at special quantity discounts for bulk purchases for sales promotions, premiums, fund-raising, and educational or institutional use.

Special book excerpts or customized printings can also be created to fit specific needs. For details, write or phone the office of the Kensington special sales manager: Kensington Publishing Corp., 850 Third Avenue, New York, NY 10022, attn: Special Sales Department, Phone: 1-800-221-2647.

Aphrodisia and the A logo Reg. U.S. Pat & TM Off.

ISBN-13: 978-0-7582-2861-1
ISBN-10: 0-7582-2861-9

First Kensington Trade Paperback Printing: December 2008

10  9  8  7  6  5  4  3  2  1

Printed in the United States of America

# Acknowledgments

There are a few people I have to thank for helping me get this story right. First and foremost is my editor, John Scognamiglio. John, thank you for your faith, and your patience. I hope I made you proud.

Another person who I owe a big thanks to is J.J. Massa: my critique partner, my friend, and master of kicking my butt. Thank you for the late nights and the support.

Delilah Devlin, I owe you a huge thanks for trying to teach me how to plot, and for sticking with me when we discovered my brain just does not work that way, no matter how hard I try.

Diva Gwen, you jumped right in when I needed you. Thank you. Erin, as always. You were there to keep me on track, and I appreciate it more than you could know.

And thank you to my brother, Shawn, for his technical expertise in making the shots hit what I was aiming at.

Many thanks to the Allure Authors, Cathryn, Myla, Delilah, Lisa, Sylvia and Vivi, for always being there to laugh, to yell, to listen and to support. You've all become very special to me, and I'm proud of our sisterhood.

# PROLOGUE

The big Montana sky was a deep and endless blue, the air crisp and clean, the surrounding silence welcome. The sun glared off the snow-covered mountains, warming his back while a chill seeped through the shooting mat he lay on over the snow. He cradled his cheek against the stock of the Timberwolf; the big .338 Lapua Magnum rested on its bipod as he lay in wait.

He concentrated on his breathing, slow and smooth, in and out, keeping his heart rate steady as he mentally rechecked his firing solution. The range 760 yards, a twenty-degree down angle gave him a corrected range of 714 yards. A few leaves rustled at the 600 yard mark, but a one-mile-per-hour wind wouldn't require a correction for the big cartridge.

The math helped him block out any distractions—including the chill from the ground and the knowledge that he wasn't the only one hunting that afternoon.

*Without Warning, Sans Remorse.* The military snipers' motto came quick and easy to his mind.

Seven hundred sixty yards away, near the far edge of the clearing slightly below him, a living, breathing, and bleeding jackrabbit was staked out. He could almost hear its cries, like the sounds of a screaming baby. The wolf *did* hear it, that's what lured him in. That, and the scent of fresh blood. It slowly inched its way around the edge of the clearing, stalking its prey.

Drake's finger tightened on the trigger, holding on the second stage as he tracked the beast's movements. It was clear this wolf was no ordinary wild animal. The size of it was a clue, but the thing that really stood out was the complete caution with which it entered the clearing. Instead of attacking the flailing rabbit, the wolf inched forward slowly, nose lifted as he scented the air, almost as if he expected a trick. Drake took up the pound of pressure on the trigger. The hand-turned silver bullet burst from the barrel—the muzzle break had worked perfectly, allowing him to watch the impact, right through the ribs of the beast. The sound of the meaty contact reached Drake's ears a couple of seconds later.

Drake stood, ran the bolt, applied the safety, folded the bipod's legs, and slung the rifle over his shoulder. With quick, sure steps he made his way off the small snow-covered boulder he'd used as a perch and through the trees. By the time he reached the clearing, the beast was gone. In its place a naked man lay on the frozen ground, little bubbles forming in the thick blood oozing from his chest as he struggled for breath.

"H-how?" he wheezed. "Why?"

Drake lowered his mental shields and reached out. Sure enough, the man's confusion was feigned. Anger and malice, cut by a cold intelligence, made it clear the man was stalling, trying to buy time for his wound to heal so he could attack Drake. Being an empath made Drake a handy human lie detector.

"Half a dozen deaths in this county, in the last three months alone, where the cause of death is listed as mauling by wild animal—dog or wolf." His voice as emotionless and blank as his expression. Drake brought the rifle up, aiming at the man's forehead. "You hunt people, *wolf*, big boys' rules."

Acceptance flickered in his target's eyes a second before Drake squeezed the trigger. Blood and brains stained the almost-pristine snow as the shot echoed across the hills.

# 1

Drake was so engrossed in the papers in front of him that he wasn't even aware of the warmth seeping into his system when it first began. Eyes flicking back and forth from papers to computer screen, mind locked onto one path, he was completely focused on the project in front of him—until the warmth turned to heat and desire washed over him, firing up his blood and making his cock swell.

Gritting his teeth, he lifted his head and scanned the room. The main office space of Hunter Protection Group resembled the bullpen of a cop shop—organized chaos. HPG employed a dozen field agents, all of them with a special talent for hunting the things that go bump in the night, plus support and technical staff. More than half of that staff was in the office that day, and all of them were giving off one emotion or another. A crowd always meant that, once Drake's attention was pulled from the task at hand, emotions came at him from all sides.

Frustration, anxiety, worry, happiness, contentment, and finally the desire. Drake had learned at a very young age to protect himself from the emotions that he felt all too easily. After thirty-plus years, keeping his psychic shields up at all times was automatic, but every now and then he slipped.

Less than five feet away Jewel Kattalis perched on the corner of his partner's desk, and Angelo Devlin, AKA "Devil," was eating the woman up with his eyes. A person didn't need to be an empath to know what the guy was thinking. Except Drake *was* an empath. So not only could he guess what Devil was thinking, he could *feel* what he was feeling.

Heat. A lot of heat, coursing through his veins and settling in his dick.

Swallowing a groan, Drake gritted his teeth and tried to get control. He closed his eyes, breathed deep, and slammed shut the psychic pathway in his mind that had eased open when he wasn't paying attention.

"You two gonna do any work or just drool over each other all day?" he practically snarled at the couple nearby.

Devil's head snapped around. "What?"

Drake glanced pointedly at the sultry brunette on the edge of the desk.

*"Get a grip, man. I can't think straight with the two of you wanting to do nothing more than fuck like hyperactive rabbits."* He sent the thought at Devil before continuing out loud. "Get out of here. I'll finish the paperwork."

Devil was a telepath so Drake's silent message got through loud and clear. He grinned and stood, grabbing Jewel by the hand and pulling her toward the door. "C'mon, babe. Drake needs some space."

The door closed behind the couple and the desire leaked slowly from Drake's system, leaving him calm . . . mostly.

Just then another agent strode past Drake's desk and a wave of anxiety swarmed him.

Fuck the paperwork, he needed to get out of there, fast. Drake shut down his computer and grabbed his jacket from the back of his chair before striding from the room without a word to anyone. He needed to find his own happy place and take the edge off the raw emotions overloading him.

Eyes closed, head bent, Drake focused on the waves of pleasure that Linda felt. They rolled over his mind, making his balls tighten and his dick even harder. His skin itched all over, and the telltale tingle between his legs grew stronger with every pump of his hips. Burying himself deep into Linda's warm, willing flesh, he reveled in her arousal.

He lowered his head, found her nipple, and sucked it between his lips. Another jolt of pleasure hit him and he sucked harder, scraping her with his teeth until her back arched and her sighs turned to moans. Soft hips moved to meet his thrusts, her pussy sucking at him each time he withdrew, her fingers digging into his back. Sliding his hand between their sweat-slicked bodies, he nudged her hard little clit and her climax crashed over them both. Her cunt clenched and sensations engulfed him, helping him ride her orgasm to his own.

Heart pounding, he rolled off the woman and basked in the blank moments of space when there was nothing but satisfaction and contentment floating around the generic hotel room.

He could've drifted right off to sleep. He was almost there when Linda rolled over, her hand trailing across his chest. It wasn't the physical touch that disturbed him, it was the longing that emanated from her that did it. She wanted more from him than he could give. Biting back a sigh, Drake raised his shields and sat up on the side of the bed.

Without a word, Linda slid from the bed and headed for the bathroom, her delicate hand trailing over his bare shoulder as she passed him. It was a familiar touch, one of commiseration and comfort, yet covetous at the same time.

He'd called on her often enough that she knew exactly how

he liked things—straightforward and simple. She'd been happy when he'd called. Not the fake "You're a regular customer" kind of happy, but truly happy.

Drake hadn't been sure if she was glad because he knew which buttons to push to get her off when she had to work a lot more to please most of her customers or because he paid her well. He hadn't really cared, either.

Women found him good looking and he would have had no trouble picking up a stranger for the night when the urge to fuck hit him, but Linda was—she'd been his haven, an uncomplicated woman who wasn't ashamed of getting paid to have sex with a select clientele and then leave them alone. But she was starting to want more.

She would never ask for anything from him—she was a professional—but she didn't have to. He felt it. And that meant he wouldn't be seeing her again.

Drake was back in the office and at his desk early the next morning. Something in the pages he'd been going over had niggled at the back of his mind all night, and he couldn't let it go.

The instant Devil and Jewel walked through the doors he called to them. "Get over here and take a look at this."

Alerted by the tone of Drake's voice, Devil quickened his step, and Jewel followed him. "What'd you find?"

Drake showed them the one gem he'd unearthed from the mountain of crap HPG had pulled from the home of the werewolf he'd taken out four days earlier. "This guy had a ton of notes on all sorts of supernatural stuff. Astrology, myths, legends . . . and this."

Devil scrutinized it for a minute but shook his head before handing it to Jewel. "What is it?"

Jewel gasped. She raised her gaze and Drake nodded. "It's

the Navajo symbol for *skinwalker*," she murmured. "What most urban legends call shape-shifters."

That got Devil's complete attention. Three months earlier, Jewel's younger sister had been kidnapped by a demon and held hostage as the *key* to open up a gateway to hell he'd built. They'd gotten her back safe and sound, but the demon had wanted Nadya because she was half pureblood shape-shifter.

The real shit thing was, no one knew what being a pureblood shape-shifter really meant. Not the gypsy caravan Jewel and Nadya were raised in, and not Devil or Drake. Worse yet, none of the many researchers employed by HPG had been able to dig up anything beyond legends.

It would be an understatement to say the last three months had been a lot of trial and error. They'd stumbled their way along, trying to figure out what exactly Nadya's powers were. And Drake, who rarely had an emotion of his own but felt everyone else's so clearly, found himself sympathizing with the tough sixteen–year-old who was scared of the unknown within herself.

This symbol, found in the home of a rogue werewolf, was their first lead to finding another shape-shifter, and maybe eventually some help for the girl.

For the next three hours they shuffled through the rest of the files and notebooks on Drake's desk. As long as they all stayed focused on the job at hand, Drake was fine, but he kept getting flashes of Jewel's excitement. It didn't matter that he was shielding himself as much as he could.

"Everything points to a *Sharza* in Chadwick," Devil said with a sigh. "Is that a nickname? A family name? We need to go check out the town and find this person. They might be able to help us understand Nadya."

Jewel raised an eyebrow at her lover, her dark eyes lighting up with temper. "Excuse me? I understand my sister just fine, thank you."

"Her powers. Help to understand her powers."

"Even if we do find them, and this person is a true skin-walker, do we really want their help?" Jewel asked, shaking her head slowly. "They use powerful black magic to take on the shape of the animals they kill. That's why we were raised to believe *all* shape-shifters are evil. I'm not so sure this is the sort of person we want helping my sister."

"I thought you said shape-shifters aren't evil. That even their 'bastard cousins,' the werewolves, weren't necessarily all bad."

Jewel's spine snapped straight and she glared at her lover. "Nadya's *not* evil."

"I'll go," Drake said, interrupting them before they could really get going. Their rising emotions were making his skin itch all over and his head was starting to ache. "I'll just go do some recon and poke around a little. You need to stick around and get the new house ready for Gina and Caleb's Christmas visit."

"You want to go alone?" Devil stared at him. "Gina will be pissed if you're not here when they arrive."

Gina was Devil's newly married kid sister, and Drake loved her like she was his own blood. He and Devil had gone through boot camp together in the military and became close friends when they realized they had more in common than just psychic abilities. When Drake had gone home with Devil one year, Gina had made him feel like another brother. And since she'd just recently learned exactly what they did for HPG, she and her new husband were going to visit *them* for the holidays for the first time.

It would be nice to share the holidays with those he considered family, but he was already getting sick of being battered by happy-happy from being around the thoroughly-in-love Devil and Jewel. Add in a set of newlyweds and he didn't know if he'd survive. Time alone before dealing with a houseful of people was very appealing, even if he'd still be working.

Shit, all he ever did was work anyway.

"I'll be back before they arrive." He met Devil's gaze. "But I could use some alone time before things get too hectic."

Understanding filled Devil's eyes. Every now and then Drake needed to get away on his own to recharge when his shields began to slip too often. When that happened, other people's emotions started to swamp him and drive him a little bit crazy. And they both knew crazy was not a good fit for him.

"I'll leave in the morning and call if I learn anything." Mind made up, he shut the lid on his laptop and grabbed his jacket from the back of his chair before striding from the room without another word.

# 2

The plan had been to leave for Chadwick in the morning, but as usual, shit happens and the plan had to be adjusted. Drake left Vancouver after dinner, not bothered at all by the thought of driving through the mountains at night.

The ten-hour drive from Vancouver, where the Hunter Protection Group offices and training compound were based, to Chadwick was nothing but peace and quiet for Drake. Driving his own truck meant he had his preferred weapons handy. It didn't matter to him that he wasn't officially on a case, he didn't like to be caught unprepared. Especially since traditional weapons weren't always of use against the things he hunted as an HPG agent.

Drake zoned out as he drove, letting his ingrained survival instinct take over while he rebuilt his psychic walls. He didn't play music, he didn't talk to himself, he didn't even think. He watched the snow fall, flicking his lights from bright to low beam depending on the road and the density of the snowfall. The roads consistently got worse as he headed deeper into the mountains, but it didn't bother him. Not much truly bothered him anymore. As long as he could just *be* without suffering other people's stray emotions, he was fine.

It was just after five in the morning when Drake took the highway turn off into the valley where the entrance to the small town of Chadwick could be found. Spread out over the bottom of the valley and continuing up the sides of the mountains and blanketed in deep fluffy snow, Chadwick was too picturesque for words, even at night. Postcard perfect, it was secluded, slightly old fashioned, and completely innocuous.

The perfect place for a shape-shifter to hide.

He checked into the only hotel he could find, ignoring the way the pretty redhead behind the desk flirted with him, and went to check out his room.

The hotel was a big, old stone structure. Obviously a heritage building, well built with solid walls and solid doors, yet well maintained and clean with an almost-homey feel. He slid his weapons bag under the bed, did a quick sweep of the room, and decided to take a look at the town before it woke up.

She knew he was there before she saw him. The crisp winter wind carried his scent, warning her that she was no longer alone in the night.

The new scent floating on the air had jolted her mind from the joy of running and brought her back to the here and now quickly. Attention tightly focused, she inched forward and crouched at the edge of the tree line to scan the surrounding area. In the dark of the night she could clearly see the building ten yards in front of her that housed both her home and her business.

Creeping through the empty yard on soft paws, she paused at the back door. She should forget about the scent and get inside undetected while she still could. As foolish as it was, she knew even as the thought entered her brain that her curiosity would win. It was the way of cats, big or small, and at that moment, she was as much cat as she was woman.

Besides, now she could hear the frosty whisper of footsteps crunching on the snow in the silent night. He wasn't as close as the wind-carried scent had first implied.

Adrenaline pumping up through her system, she made her way along the side of the building, keeping close to the brick walls so she stayed in the shadow of the street lamp when she peered around the corner. It was a bit of a risk, but chance was on her side. He wouldn't spot her.

There he was—less than half a block away and heading in her direction. She watched as the stranger walked up the deserted main street of Chadwick.

The rhythm of his gait and the way he constantly checked his surroundings put her nerves on edge. Smooth and relaxed, yet with a sharp awareness that radiated off the man while his head swung from side to side as if he were searching for something. Or worse, *hunting* something.

Her heart jackhammered in her chest. Melissa Montrose was not fond of hunters.

The pitch-black night made him look so . . . alone. No, that's not right. The closer he got, the more she saw, and she knew it wasn't only darkness and the quiet of the night that made him seem so. It was something about *him*. Melissa got the sense that even in the middle of a crowd, that man was alone.

He stopped in front of the bookstore below her apartment, and a shiver rippled down her spine. For a moment he just looked in the bookstore window, then his head swung around, his gaze landing unerringly on the corner she peeked around.

Melissa froze, her breath catching in her throat as anticipation flooded her veins. As long as she didn't move, there was no way he would see her in the shadow. But she saw him clearly, and her disquiet took on a new edge. Danger. Her insides quivered and a new, elemental tension coiled low in her belly.

He was pure, powerful, alpha, and she wanted him.

The stranger shook his head, then turned and moved back toward the center of town—and she found herself almost wishing he had seen her.

She gave her own head a shake, then made her way to the back door of the building. She shouldn't want him. Hot and sexy was good—Melissa could use some hot and sexy in her life that wasn't self-induced. Mysterious—not so much. Mysterious made her . . . antsy. Danger was one thing. Risk was something else entirely.

Yep, the man was dangerous.

Especially since he prowled the empty streets in the middle of the night. Sure, she'd been prowling the forest in the middle of the night, but she was different.

Melissa paused at the back door to take one last look around, ensuring she was indeed alone. Then, with nothing more than a thought, magic swept through her and she shifted, leaving the winter lynx behind. Naked skin pebbling in the chill air, Melissa entered the building as a young woman.

*Thank God the people of Chadwick didn't know how truly different she was.*

# 3

She was every inch of his adolescent fantasies. From her sleek little body with lush curves in all the right places to her long hair pulled back in a tight bun.

Drake watched the woman stride down the aisle between tall stacks of the bookstore and struggled to regain some of his standard detachment. She was coming his way, but because her eyes were buried in the book in her hands, she hadn't noticed him yet. This gave him complete freedom to drink in the sight of her.

She had a woman's body, soft and curvy in all the right places, with a subtle, underlying strength. And at that moment, her delectable form was covered in a simple white button-up blouse that skimmed breasts so full his mouth watered and a short, fitted skirt that clung to rounded hips. Those luscious, rounded hips led to the kind of legs that would wrap around a man and hold him tight while he fucked her raw. Drake swallowed to keep from drooling. He was a grown man, after all.

He couldn't help but look . . . and look again. It wasn't just her body or the way her clothes fit that had his dick jumping. It was the neat and pressed look of her while being surrounded by shelves of books, caramel-colored hair pulled back and nose buried in a book. Drake's balls grew heavy and hot blood rushed through his veins. She looked like the strict and sexy librarian, and he wanted desperately to be the naughty schoolboy called into her office.

As if sensing his gaze on her, she glanced up and stopped dead. Apprehension skittered across her face and was gone so fast Drake wondered if he imagined it.

"Well, hel-lo," she said, her smile flirtatious. "You're new in town."

"Just visiting."

"Winters tend to isolate us up here in the mountains. We don't get many visitors this time of year."

"I like isolation," he said as he scanned the small store. He ignored the subtle invitation for conversation and fought to get rid of the image of pinning her body against the wall and rucking her skirt up until he reached hot, wet woman. Jerking his gaze from her, he moved farther inside the store and fingered a chunk of obsidian that was part of a display on the table against the wall.

Hyperaware of her, he knew the moment the female shifted her weight and refocused on him. "You said you were visiting. Do you have family here? Friends you came to spend the holidays with?"

"No."

She tilted her head, eyes narrowing on him. "You don't talk much, do you?"

Before he could stop himself, one corner of his mouth lifted in a half smile. "Words are often overrated."

"That's the wrong thing to say if you're trying to get on the good side of a bookstore owner."

Her dark eyes twinkled and the stern tone of her voice went

straight to his dick. He had to fight to keep from making his librarian fantasy a reality. She was strong and confident, and so damn sexy he couldn't resist. "Who said I was trying to get on your good side?"

His blood heated and his mind slowed as she pointedly looked down and then up his body, taking her time. Careful. Slow. Obvious. The deliberate inspection had him fighting the urge to strip down and bare himself to her. Christ! What was going on with him?

"*You* should be," she said, tossing the words over her shoulder as she turned and stepped behind the sales counter. "My good side can be a lot of fun."

*Oh, I bet*, Drake thought. His system was alive and tingling from the going-over she'd given him.

Drake had honed his control to a lethal edge over the years. He wasn't an adolescent boy whose emotions or hormones controlled him. Which was why his elemental response to her was so shocking.

By the time she was behind the counter, Drake had his desire under control. Or so he thought. She turned and asked, "Is there anything I can do for you?" and a ripple of pure yearning went through him.

Fuck, if he was getting this turned on with his shields up, letting them down would be sure to take them both on a wild, wild ride. Her emotions would flood his senses, feeding his own desires, and he'd be bending her over that sales counter within seconds.

Dropping his shields and immersing himself in her passion was something he actually *eager* to do. It had been a long time since he wanted to bed a woman for pleasure, and not just for release. A long night between her legs would be a great way to relax—and maybe even learn some of the town's secrets. *Sure, why not?*

He stepped up to the counter. "Have dinner with me."

Her brows jumped in surprise and her lips twitched. "Changed your mind?" she asked, her eyes sparkling with silent mirth.

It took him a second, but his brain soon caught up to the conversation.

"Okay," he said. She was sharp, and he was surprised at how much that pleased him. "What *would* be the right thing to say to get on your good side?"

A dimple flashed in her cheek. "You can start with telling me your name."

"Drake Wheeler." He held out a hand. "And you are?"

Her palm slid against his and he was surprised there wasn't a visible spark at the skin-on-skin contact. "Melissa Montrose, and I'm sorry, I already have plans for tonight. Another time?"

"Tomorrow," he said.

Melissa's full lips twitch turned into a full-blown grin at his abrupt demand, and he groaned mentally. His brain had disengaged and the word had popped out his mouth without any guidance from him.

She nodded and replied as if he hadn't just made an idiot of himself. "Dinner tomorrow night would be nice."

If the tension snapping between them was any indication, *nice* would be way too mild a word to describe any time they spent together. Incendiary was more like it.

"I'll talk to you tomorrow then," he said with a tight smile before turning on his heel and leaving. It wasn't until he got bitch-slapped by the frigid wind outside that he realized he'd left the store without even taking a look around.

A hot flash whipped through Melissa as she mentally replayed the moment she'd first looked up and spotted Drake inside her bookstore. He was big. Not just tall, but big and *built*.

At five foot five she wasn't super tiny or anything, but he had to be close to a foot taller than her! Saliva had literally pooled in her mouth at the true breadth of the man's shoulders when he'd unzipped his Gore-Tex jacket.

All she'd wanted to do was curl up at his side, under his arm, and run her hands over his muscled chest and flat abs. And that was so unlike her! Cuddling had never been her thing.

She'd looked him up and down, over said stomach and then down below the belt, and all thoughts of him prowling the streets in the early morning darkness had fled. The black cargo-style pants he'd worn were a bit loose, but fitted enough for her to see he was probably built there as well.

Bookworm she might be, celibate she was not, at least not by choice. Living in such a small town narrowed her catalog of erotic entertainment drastically. The big guy was hot, and she was horny. One way to solve the mysterious aspect of him was to get closer—a lot closer. And she knew just the way to do that.

Drake played small-town tourist all afternoon. He spent some time in every store on Main Street, pretending to browse the merchandise when he was really checking out the people. From what he'd seen so far, Melissa hadn't been lying about Chadwick not having many visitors this time of year. Even though Christmas was less than two weeks away, he didn't see many people who felt like visitors.

This was a good and a bad thing. Good because it ensured Chadwick was calm and tranquil, exactly what he needed to recharge. Not so good because it meant he, a stranger in the small town, would stand out.

He'd been in the diner for almost two hours and the supper rush was over. Done eating, he sat back against the padded bench and people watched. He pretended to read the local paper, but more often than not he was reading the emotions of the people coming and going in the comfortable little eatery.

Food sources, be it a diner or marketplace, were often the best venue to get a feel for a place, but Drake hadn't read or sensed anything unusual in Chadwick's shopkeepers that day, and the same for the residents that had entered the diner so far. This was okay since he wasn't in any hurry. He was thinking of the recon trip as a semiholiday.

The bell above the diner entrance jangled loudly and a woman wearing nothing but jeans and a sweater rushed in on a gust of frigid air. Immediately, Drake's pulse jumped and his skin tightened as a tingle of awareness rippled through him. Melissa.

Unable to look away, he tracked her as she strode confidently to the counter, her high-heeled boots clicking loudly against the laminate flooring.

"Melissa Montrose!" The silver-haired waitress by the cash register raised a hand in greeting, scolding at the same time. "What are you doing running about without a coat on? You're going to catch your death."

"I was outside for a whole ninety seconds, Mary," she shot back. "If I can't handle that, I don't deserve to call myself a Canadian."

Mary grumbled good-naturedly.

She'd changed clothes. Gone was the sexy librarian and in her place was a sexy goddess in casual jeans and a thick wool sweater. Melissa leaned forward and grabbed some extra napkins from behind the counter as her food was being rung up, and the faded denim stretched across her shapely ass. The almost-unbearable urge to cover her had Drake's thighs bunching under the table. He wanted his chest against her back and his legs tucked up behind hers while he claimed her from behind.

As if sensing his thoughts, she straightened up and looked over her shoulder, catching his stare. She quirked an eyebrow and he met her gaze head-on. The view had been nice; he wasn't going to apologize for enjoying it.

"Here you go. Now hurry back to your place and enjoy your dinner."

"Oh, I will." She picked up the bag of food and headed toward the door, a spark in her eye as she looked right at him. "I'm *very* hungry."

Suddenly Drake was hungry too, and not for food.

Melissa dashed home with her bag full of food and a grin on her face. Seeing Drake in the diner had been a stroke of pure luck. She hadn't been able to stop thinking about him all day.

It hadn't helped when her best friend had stopped in the store to tell her about the new stud that had checked into the hotel early that morning.

"You should see him, Mel. He's big, but not big like a muscle head bodybuilder—you can tell he's got a rock'n body though . . . Did I mention big?" Erin asked with a suggestive wiggle of her eyebrows.

Melissa had laughed. "Yes, you mentioned big."

She hadn't yet told her friend that she'd met the stranger already, and that gave her pause. Erin was like a sister to her. They'd been best friends since they were kids, a bond that had only strengthened as the years passed and both of them lost family.

Instead of talking to Erin about seeing Drake walk the streets while the town still slept or his coming into the store that day, she'd cut her friend's comments short and told her they'd talk that night.

Now, as Mel strolled into her apartment, she hoped Erin had

forgotten about Drake. For some reason, she wanted to keep her meeting with him to herself for a while longer.

Erin was already there. "Geez, did you get enough food?" she said when she saw the bag Mel was carrying.

"I'm hungry."

"You're always hungry."

Mel shrugged. This was true.

Erin got plates and silverware and brought them to the table while Mel began to unpack the ribs and french fries, her stomach rumbling at the scent of barbeque. "So how's Troy?" she asked before Erin could bring up the subject of the new stud in town again.

"He's still in Colorado getting ready for the NorAm Cup competition."

"When does he get back?" Erin's on-again, off-again lover was a professional snowboarder and in the winter months he lived and breathed the competition circuit.

"I don't know. Probably not until April he said."

Mel froze. "He's not coming home for Christmas?"

"Not this year." Erin picked up her plate of food and headed for the living room, leaving Mel to follow.

Melissa bit the inside of her cheek, unsure of what to say to that. Erin and Troy were having a few relationship issues, and she really wanted to be there for her closest friend, but what she had to say wasn't what Erin would want to hear.

Ah, hell. That had never stopped her before. "I don't get why you don't just dump him and move on. He's not good enough for you."

Erin grimaced. "You've been holding that back for a while."

"I love you, Erin," she said, perching on the sofa next to her. If you couldn't talk to your best friend, who could you talk to? Besides, neither of them had any family left, so it was up to them to look after each other. "And Troy used to make you happy, but he doesn't do that anymore."

"He does make me happy!" Erin's objection sounded a little flat.

"When he's here."

Erin nodded, her smile wry. "When he's here."

Mel chewed some meat off one of her ribs, silent, thinking. Letting Erin think. When the rib was clean to the bone, she spoke again. "All you've ever wanted was to get married and have a family, Erin. To be a mom. You can't do that with a guy who won't even come home for Christmas holidays."

"He's got a competition."

"There's *no* competition until January, and you know it."

Mel's heart ached at the sight of Erin's big, brown puppy dog eyes, filled with uncertainty. She opened her mouth again but before she could say anything else, Erin pointed to the television where Dwayne Johnson had just walked on screen. "Enough talk. Let's just watch the movie."

Biting her tongue, Melissa turned her eyes to the TV where the sight of the ex-wrestler brought Drake right back into her head.

# 4

Drake woke up with a killer hard-on. Not the normal, half-hard lazy kind either. Before he even opened his eyes he was aware of the hot blood filling his dick and making it throb to the beat of his heart. Without thought he palmed his shaft and began to stroke. There was no soft touch, no gentle tease. His grip was firm and his strokes sure as he pumped his fist up and down. Everything was centered on his groin and pre-come oozed from the slit at the tip. His thumb skimmed over the top and he gasped at the sensation that ripped through him.

The image of Melissa filled his mind. She was on her knees in front of him, her lips wrapped around his cock, her nails digging into his naked thighs as she worked him over. She'd be good at it, he knew it. Her wide eyes looking up at him as she cupped his balls, her tongue swirling around the head, her lips shiny and slick as they moved up and down his shaft. It was too much for him, the sight of her, the feel of her, the sensations as fire rushed through him and pooled in his cock. He was going to explode.

His fist tightened and he focused on the ridge under the

head. He was whole-handing it now, fingers curled, palm cupping and caressing the sensitive head with each stroke, tighter, faster. His chest heaved as he fought for breath, and in his mind he saw his hands sink into a cloud of caramel hair as he took charge. He cupped Melissa's head and held her still as he began to fuck her willing mouth. His cock throbbed, his back arched, and his hips lifted off the bed as a groan tore from his throat and pleasure ripped through him, spewing from his body in a hot stream that hit his chest and belly.

Seconds later his brain came back online and his eyes popped open. Holy Christ! He couldn't remember the last time he'd felt pleasure like that, with or without a woman.

Shit, when he jerked off it was more because his body demanded it, needed it. It was a release, not an enjoyment thing. Not this time though. Stunned, he realized that the pleasure, the emotion, that he'd just felt, had been all his. And it was because of the woman in his fantasy.

Groaning to himself, he pushed the woman and the fantasy from his mind and climbed from the sheets that had tangled around his thighs. Time to start the day.

He spent the morning in his hotel room, working on his laptop, going through files again, and trading e-mails with Devil. After a couple of hours digging in Chadwick's city archives, he shut the computer down and headed back to the Main Street Diner for lunch.

Mary, the same silver-haired matron from the night before, was working the counter. He sat down, ordered, and listened for the next hour as she joked with the men and gossiped with the women who came and went.

Doing his best to ignore any lingering thoughts of Melissa, he ate his burger and waited until the diner emptied out a bit.

When things had slowed down enough, he smiled and called Mary over.

He pulled out the charm and smiled at the older lady. "I was hoping you could help me out, Mary.".

Devil had checked phone books and the Internet for a "Sharza" when they'd been going over all the data that last day in the office, and he'd found nothing. But in a town like Chadwick, there was no better fount of information than a woman with a taste for gossip.

"What can I do for you, young man?" she asked, wiping her hands on a bright pink dishcloth.

"I've lost touch with an old friend. Last I knew he lived here in Chadwick, but I haven't had any luck with directories or Internet searches. It occurred to me that you might know of him or his family."

She snorted. "You young people put way too much stock in all those electronic gadgets. Who are you looking for, son?"

"Sharza," he said. Pulling a name out of thin air he continued. "Bill Sharza."

Mary's eyes glazed over for a minute as she thought hard. Drake opened his senses but felt nothing more than curiosity and a general sense of happiness.

"No," she said, shaking her head. "Don't know anyone by that name. Sorry."

Drake nodded. "Do have any other ideas on who I could ask, or where I could look for family records, maybe of the surrounding areas?"

"I've lived in this town my whole life, I'm fourth generation y'know?" Mary said with a proud grin. "My great-great-great grandparents had the first diner right on this spot. The town grew up around us. If there was anyone with that name in Chadwick, I'd know it."

He thanked her and put up with some general small talk until he finished his coffee.

Clear blue skies and bright sunshine didn't take away from the chilly December day. The air was cold enough that his breath could be seen in the air as Drake made his way back to the bookstore. Something about the store had set off his radar on his early morning walk the day before, and once he got past the distraction of Melissa, the need to take a deeper look was still there.

Pushing open the door he stepped into the bookstore, surprised when he didn't immediately see Melissa. Then a cry of "I'll be there in a moment," came from the rear of the store.

Without thought, Drake followed her voice and found Melissa brushing her knees off as she straightened up from the floor. His fantasy image of her on her knees flashed in his head and his whole body hardened.

He strode forward and she looked up with a pleasant smile. The smile wilted and her dark eyes lit up as he got closer and she noted the intent in his gaze. He stopped when their bodies were separated by mere inches, and electricity snapped between them. All the little hairs on Drake's body stood on end and he beat down the need to pin her up against the wall and make her his.

"Hi," she said, her voice more breathless than he remembered.

He said nothing, just leaned closer and breathed deep, inhaling her scent. Her warm, spicy, very *female* scent. Tearing his gaze from her face he noted the hard, pointed tips of her breasts pressing against her thin T-shirt. He also saw the beat of her pulse hammering at the base of her throat.

"Drake." His name was barely a breath from her lips. He raised his eyes and lowered his head toward the lush lips that had given him such pleasure in his dreams.

The loud clang of the bell above her door sounded again, pulling Drake up short. "Delivery!"

A low groan escaped Drake and he clamped his mouth shut. He wasn't sure if he should be thankful for the interruption or if he should go kill the delivery guy.

Melissa's lips opened and closed, her hands poised above his chest. "Ugh!" She shook her head, finally calling out, "I'll be right there!"

Drake stepped back an inch, still silent.

"We're still on for tonight, right?" she asked.

He nodded, not bothering to hide the intent he knew was stamped on his features. "Oh, yeah."

"Good," she said as she stepped past him and made her way to the front.

Drake took a deep breath and tried to shake off the intense need that had gripped him when he'd spotted Melissa. After tamping down the fierce desire surging about inside he pretended to browse the shelves. Even while his brain catalogued the layout and specifications of the store, his gaze kept snapping back to the woman at the front of the store like an elastic band stretched to its limit.

"Get a grip, man," he muttered to himself.

Scattered among the books were various small displays of jewelry and incense, along with handmade soaps and candles. There was even a small rack in the back corner of the store that held a bunch of bags and purses for sale. And next to that rack was a closed door.

Looking at that door, Drake knew it would lead to more than a storage room. Someone lived above the store, and that someone had been watching him hours earlier when he'd done his first walk-through of the town.

From between the shelves of the bookrack, he could see her at the counter. The delivery guy was long gone and she sat on a stool, working on a laptop, studiously ignoring him. Yet his instincts told him she was as aware of him as he was of her. Maybe it had been her watching him. There was certainly something different about her.

Different enough that she could be who he was looking for?

He braced himself and started to lower his psychic shields just as the glass door at the front of the store swung open again and the redheaded sprite from the hotel burst into the store.

"Did you meet him?" she asked as she unwrapped her scarf and bounced behind the sales counter. She set down a cardboard tray with a paper bag and a couple of Styrofoam coffee cups on it and pulled up a stool next to Melissa. "I saw him heading this way from the hotel, and it just about killed me not to call you. So? Did the hot and sexy stud come by here yet? Give me the deets, woman!"

Melissa's laugh danced through the air and Drake found himself smiling at the sound of it. "He's still here, Erin."

"Oops!"

The little redhead glanced his way and he concentrated on the book in front of him, pretending he hadn't heard them. Then he noticed the title of the book and all thoughts of the two women disappeared.

*Hunt for the Skinwalker.*

Drake glanced at the books on either side of it, and saw a shitload of titles about skinwalkers and werewolves, along with some others about tarot cards, dream readings, and even a manual on how to enhance your psychic abilities.

He bit back a snort of laughter. Why were there never books on how to dull your psychic abilities?

There had been crystals at the front of the store, too. His brain kicked into high gear, thinking, reasoning, theorizing. New Age spiritualism, the occult, and the paranormal would always have followers. It made sense for the store to have books on the subjects, but Drake's radar was humming. He was on to something.

Paperback in hand, he strolled up to the counter and interrupted the women's whispering. The last thing he needed was a book on skinwalkers, he knew all he needed to from Jewel and the HPG researchers, but he really wanted to see Melissa's reaction to it.

"Hey, Mr. Wheeler," the redhead said with a grin when he stopped in front of her.

"Hello, Erin. Done with work for the day?"

"I wish. If I was done work, I'd be out there with my snowboard." She jerked her chin in the direction of the snow-covered mountain out the window. "I'm on the early shift this week—which is why I was there when you checked in at that ungodly hour yesterday. So, I'm just on a lunch break."

Finished being polite, he handed the paperback to Melissa to ring up and watched for a reaction. She glanced at the title and smiled as she told him the amount, the only outward reaction a slight widening of her eyes. He lowered his shields a little and was awash in the sad resignation radiating from Erin.

He glanced at her and she smiled at him brightly.

*People are weird*, he thought.

Pushing aside Erin's emotions he lowered his shields further and reached out to Melissa specifically . . . and found nothing.

*What the fuck?*

"Here you go," Melissa said, holding a small plastic bag out to him.

"Thanks." He took the bag she held and gave her an automatic smile as his mind raced. "I'll see you tonight."

She threw a quick glance at Erin and nodded. "I should be there a couple of minutes after eight."

He nodded and left the store, already trying to figure out why he couldn't pick up any emotions from Melissa.

# 5

"See you tonight?"

Mel laughed at Erin's open envy. "He asked if I wanted to have dinner. I said yes."

"I hate you."

"Don't pout, Erin. It makes you look like you're twelve years old. Besides, you don't really want him. He'd crush you."

Erin wiggled her eyebrows and leered. "Not if I was on top."

They laughed, unwrapping the submarine sandwiches Erin had brought over from the hotel for lunch. Erin was one of those women who'd look forever young, especially because she was so petite, but her cute and innocent look was deceiving. When she was forty she'd be glad of it, but at twenty-eight, it wasn't something she loved about herself.

"So, talk." Erin picked up her sandwich, eyeing Melissa over the bulging half loaf. "Tell me what you know about Mr. Yummy."

Heat flooded her cheeks as she remembered the way her body had instantly responded to Drake's nearness.

When she'd stood up and their gazes had locked, tension

had flooded her entire system at the predatory look in his intense emerald eyes and she knew she was on a slippery slope. He was definitely hunting her. She just wasn't sure if it was in the way all men hunted women, or if it was because he knew what she was.

"What's to tell? You said it yourself. He's a hot and sexy stranger. And I, for one, could use some hot and sexy fun."

"That's it?" Erin asked around a mouthful of food.

"Yep."

"You suck."

Mel flashed a wicked grin, falling into the easy camaraderie she'd shared with Erin since grade school. "I just might. It all depends on what he has to offer."

Erin groaned. "Enough talk about sex. It's been too long for me and the batteries in my vibrator are dead."

Melissa bit the inside of her cheek. She was surprised when Erin glanced at her over a piece of lettuce and sighed. "It's probably going to be even longer since I called Troy after I left your place last night to tell him I wanted to break up."

"Really?"

Erin nodded.

Now that her attention was totally focused on Erin, Mel could sense a difference in her energy. She seemed more relaxed, if still a bit down. "How do you feel?"

"I thought about everything you said last night, well, I've been thinking about it for a while now, and I guess I have to admit that I've been holding on to Troy because my parents loved him so much too."

Erin's parents had been killed in an avalanche three years earlier. They'd been outdoor adventure lovers, just like Erin and Troy, and the four of them had often spent time hiking or skiing on the mountain together. It made sense that Erin would want to hang on to her relationship with Troy because of the family memories.

Mel slid off her stool and put her arms around her friend. "You and Troy will always be friends," she said. "You've been through too much together to *not* be. It's just time to find romance with someone else."

"You're right." Erin squeezed her and then pulled back. "You're always right."

Mel laughed, swallowing the lump in her throat. "I'm glad you realize that."

"So how did he take it?"

"I haven't told him yet," she said with a grimace. "He didn't answer so I just left a message for him to call me tonight."

"Oh, Erin." Having finally made the choice to break up, yet not being able to do it had to suck.

"Enough! I don't want to think about Troy anymore," she ordered. Her lips lifted in a devilish smile that almost made it to her eyes. "Distract me. What did you and the hot and sexy stud talk about before he asked you out?"

The question made Mel feel like shit for not telling Erin she'd met Drake the day before, but she still felt the need to keep the fierceness of her attraction to the man a secret. Her blood heated as an image of Drake Wheeler's forceful gaze and his silent mouth lowering toward hers filled her mind. The big guy was potent, there was no two ways about it.

"Hel-lo?" Erin waved a dainty hand in front of Melissa's face. "You still in there?"

Her spine snapped straight. "Of course," she said. "We didn't really talk about anything."

"He just walked in here and asked you out?"

Melissa smirked to hide the blush she felt rising in her cheeks. "It's all about the unspoken communication. You notice how quiet the guy is? Getting him to speak in full sentences wasn't easy."

Erin leered. "Big, blond, and dumb?"

"No." Mel shook her head. Her sandwich forgotten in her hand, she remembered what he looked like on the street in the early morning hours and goose bumps raised up on her skin. "I'm pretty sure this guy isn't dumb."

Erin's brow puckered, making her concern clear. "What do you think of the book he picked up?"

"I'm not sure what to think. It doesn't feel like a coincidence, but it's been decades since my kind has been hunted."

"That's because there's not many of your kind left to hunt, my dear."

"I also don't *feel* threatened by him," she stressed.

Erin snorted. "That's because your hormones are running amok. You need a good night with a hard man, and that's cool. Just don't check your brain at the bedroom door."

Melissa took in Erin's stern glare. Teenaged Erin might not have believed Mel when she'd first told her she was a shapeshifter with magic in her blood, but she'd been a good-enough friend to stay with her on the full moon after her sixteenth birthday, just because she'd known how worried Mel was about it.

When she'd come into her powers and Erin had witnessed it, Mel thought she might lose her best friend forever. Instead, her secret had only strengthened their friendship.

Erin would always have Melissa's back, and because of that, Melissa was brave. An irrational hunger had her insides quivering with the need to get naked and naughty with Drake. And what better way to solve the "mysterious" aspect of him than to get closer—a lot closer.

She'd have dinner with the sexy stranger, but she wouldn't forget that there was no such thing as coincidence.

\* \* \*

Hours later Melissa flipped the sign on the door and locked up the store for the night. Technically it should've remained open for another fifteen minutes, but one of the perks of owning her own business was the ability to open late, or close early, as she pleased. Especially in a small town like Chadwick. The GONE HIKING sign went up on the door at least once a week when she either opened late or closed early so she could take off up the mountain trail behind the building.

This time she was closing early so she could change for her dinner with Drake. The T-shirt and plain black slacks had been good for a day in the store, but she needed something a little— all right, a *lot* sexier—if she wanted to end the night with some adult games of the erotic sort.

She trotted up the stairs at the back of the storage room and entered her apartment over the store, her mind wandering back to her conversation with Erin, and Erin herself.

As much as Mel knew she'd sort of pushed Erin into her decision, the genuine smile and the new sense of positive energy she sported when she'd left after lunch had told Mel she'd done the right thing.

Toeing off her shoes, she left her laptop on the kitchen table and headed for her bedroom. She was so intent on her quick-change plan that she wasn't even aware something was off until she was stripped down and standing in front of the closet.

Everything looked the way it should, but the energy of the room felt wrong. Dropping the jeans she'd grabbed from the floor, she moved to her bedroom door in her underwear. Everything looked fine. Slightly messy, but that wasn't unusual.

"Paranoid much?" she muttered to herself.

No, she wasn't paranoid. Melissa had learned early on in life that she had instincts for a reason. Ignoring them could be dangerous not only to her but to many others.

39

Unable to ignore the sense that someone had invaded her territory, she prowled the apartment in search of a concrete sign. No strange scent hovered in the air and everything was where she'd left it—nothing was missing, and nothing had been moved. She found no *real* sign that someone had been in her place.

Mind swirling with possibilities, she went back to her room and made quick work of getting dressed.

Five minutes later, she was wearing low-rise black denim jeans that flattered her butt and a cashmere V-neck sweater that showed off her cleavage as she made her way back to the door. It would've been nice to wear a skirt and a garter belt with no panties to make her feel ultranaughty, but she wasn't stupid. Freezing her bits off in the December cold was not appealing.

She pulled on her boots, then stood at the big gilded mirror in the hall, unbraiding her hair before running her fingers through it until she was happy enough. She snatched up her keys from her throw-all table under the mirror, pulled on her jacket, and headed out. Hopefully the just-out-of-bed tousled look would tell Drake exactly what her intentions were.

Instead of spending more time in town, Drake had left the bookstore and followed a well-worn trail into the trees at the end of the street. Within moments the thick lodgepole pine had surrounded him, with a few Douglas fir trees to help hold the world at bay. The peace and tranquility of the forest, away from any and all people, had been perfect.

After hiking for a bit he'd been able to completely drop his shields and just relax. The only sounds he'd heard was the rustle of the tree branches when a gust of wind came along and the crunch of snow under his boots. He'd developed a rhythm to his steps and was high on the mountain in little time.

Animal tracks were more plentiful the higher he got. He saw

rabbit, deer, elk, and coyote tracks, as well as some cat ones with the telltale dimple in the top of the pad. They resembled a cougar print, but smaller, and Drake wondered if they were truly animal prints, or maybe shape-shifter.

He'd reached a clearing and stood for a bit, not thinking, not feeling anything, just relaxing and breathing in the fresh air. A layer of frost was starting to build in his lungs, so after a few more moments of peace he turned and headed back down. By the time he'd reached the hotel his ears were frozen and he hadn't been able to feel his fingertips anymore.

An hour-long hot shower had defrosted him and he was ready to eat. Even more ready to spend some more time with the sultry and surprising Melissa Montrose.

She'd lingered in the back of his mind all day and he was shocked at how hard and fast desire hit him when he thought of her. Even more amazing than the speed was the knowledge that it was his own desire he was experiencing. Since he hadn't been able to get anything from her, it had to be.

He scowled at the half-empty beer on the table in front of him as he waited for her to show up for their date. He hadn't been able to read her!

There was the possibility he hadn't been able to get anything off Melissa because Erin's emotions had been broadcasting so loud. A very slim possibility.

Ah, fuck. There was no possibility of that.

Drake had never met a person he couldn't read. Some people were harder than others, but he'd never been completely blocked before. The fact that Nadya was one of those who were a bit harder to read than most told Drake he just might've found the person he'd been looking for. It didn't matter that he'd never had a problem reading werewolves, witches, or any other supernatural creatures. What mattered was that if Nadya was hard to read and she was half pureblood, it would make sense that full purebloods would have psychic walls that much harder to breach. Like Melissa's.

Drake sighed. If any of this shit made sense.

He still couldn't figure where the name Sharza fit though. Mary had been adamant that there had been no family named Sharza to ever live in Chadwick and he believed her. But names weren't hard to change. Montrose could be an assumed name, or she might even have been adopted, like he'd been. He'd taken his own name back when he was eighteen because he'd never truly felt a part of the family that had taken him in, but maybe Melissa hadn't. Maybe her birth name was Sharza.

It added up. Probability said Melissa was a shape-shifter.

Or, maybe the werewolf had been wrong about Sharza being in Chadwick and Drake had just lucked into finding Melissa. Maybe she *wasn't* a shape-shifter.

He shook his head. *Christ, what a mess.* One thing he knew for sure, she wasn't a skinwalker. He'd flipped through the book he'd bought that afternoon, more out of curiosity than anything, and it had re-enforced everything the researched had told him. Shape-shifter, maybe. Evil skinwalker who did blood magic in order to gain powers, nope.

The heavy wooden door to the hotel's pub swung open and Melissa strode in, searching the dark interior for him. A punch of lust hit him straight in the gut and he bit back a curse.

What was it about that woman that made him feel so out of control?

"Hey there," she said when she stopped next to the booth he was in. She shook the down-filled jacket from her shoulders and he clenched his hands beneath the table to keep from reaching out and pulling her down to sit on his lap.

"Hey," he replied as she slid into the benchseat across from him.

They sat and looked at each other for a minute, neither

speaking. The air between them thickened, growing heavy with expectation, and so did his dick.

Across from him sat a female flashing cleavage and heat, and his body responded full force. He might not be able to feel her emotions, but the invitation was clear in her gaze.

"Hey, Mel. How are you doing?" The waitress stepped up to the table, breaking the tension. "You want a beer?"

"Yes, please, Terry. Thanks." She smiled at the waitress. "How's Bobby?"

Drake tuned out the conversation as they chatted briefly about the woman's family and just watched Melissa. Never one to give up, he focused his powers and pushed particularly hard at whatever was blocking him from her emotions. Her eyes flicked in his direction, as if she'd felt him, and he bit back a triumphant smile.

Oh yeah. There was definitely something *special* about her.

"So, how's your holiday going so far?" she asked him when the waitress left.

"So far, very good. The town is quiet and peaceful, the mountains are amazing, and the local scenery"—he dipped his head so she understood he was speaking of her—"is beautiful."

The slight blush that colored her cheeks told him she understood his compliment. He could be charming when he needed to be.

"And you? How was your afternoon in the bookstore?"

"Quiet. But like I said, Chadwick is pretty isolated in the winter so I'm used to it, especially this time of year."

"Tell me about yourself," he commanded. "How'd you come to be running a bookstore? And why Chadwick? Are you from around here?"

Her drink arrived and Terry asked if they were ready to order. Melissa ordered a steak with a loaded baked potato, and Drake was strangely pleased to see she wasn't going to try and be dainty with a wimpy salad. A woman with an appetite appealed to him. It made him wonder how big her other appetites were.

"I'll have the same," he told the waitress.

"Born elsewhere and raised in these mountains," Melissa answered after the waitress walked away, as if there hadn't been any interruption. "My family has been here for a few generations though. Ten years ago, my grandmother passed away and left me the family business. What about you?" She leaned forward, and Drake's eyes dropped to the fabulous cleavage she showed off.

Damn, he wanted to get his hands on those. His mouth, too. He wanted to get her all worked up, then lick the sweat off her skin before sliding his cock between the fleshy mounds and pumping until she wore a pearl necklace.

"Hel-looo?"

Drake raised his gaze, not bothering to hide the thoughts that had carried his mind away from their conversation.

Her lips turned up slightly. "I guess it's safe to say you're a breast man, eh?"

"You have a very nice figure," he said with a shrug. It was true. She had an *outstanding figure*.

She threw back her head and laughed. "Such a gentlemanly way of putting it."

A smile twitched at his mouth. She had a good laugh. Deep and full-throated. Unrestrained.

Christ, he wanted her! Everything about her made him hard.

"I was asking about you," she said, after taking a drink from her beer. "Where do you call home? What do you do for a living?"

He mentally replayed what she'd been saying before he'd gotten distracted. She was born and raised there in Chadwick.

Montrose was obviously her true name then, which meant she *might not* be who he was looking for.

Then again, that could be a good thing considering what he wanted to do to her. "I'm a security consultant for a privately owned company based out of Vancouver. We work jobs all over the world, so I travel a lot."

"That explains a few things."

He raised an eyebrow. "Yeah?"

"You have that constant readiness thing that a lot of cops have." She grinned, a teasing light in her sparkling eyes. "Plus your less–than-talkative style suits the big, tough-guy image."

"Hey, I'm talking!"

"Yes." She nodded. "Yes, you are. *Now.*" And WOW what it was doing to her. Every time he spoke his rich voice skipped over her skin, raising every tiny hair on her body and making her itch to be stroked all over.

"What can I say?" He shrugged his broad shoulders. "I'm better with action than words."

A shiver danced down her spine. She could believe it.

He was so in control and reserved—except for the heat in his eyes. Those emerald orbs burned with a flame so hot she was surprised her skin wasn't blistering everywhere he looked. But what really set her heart to pounding and her pussy to throbbing was the thought of making him lose that control. To have his big powerful body over hers, driving deep and true between her thighs would be heaven. And his hands. Oh Lordy, his hands. The sight of his long blunt fingers caressing the beer in front of him, trailing through the condensation on the glass before he'd lift it to his mouth, had her wondering how it would feel to have those fingers stroking between her thighs. Caressing, teasing, plunging. *Oh yeah.*

Not to mention that she had to struggle to keep her mind on the conversation because he kept his other hand out of sight beneath the table. He had two very fine, workable hands—she knew that from his time in the bookstore—but that hand being under the table had her mind sinking even more into the erotic arena she loved as she imagined he was doing something very naughty down below—and she so wanted to help.

Just as she was about to ask what he was doing beneath the table, their food arrived.

Silence descended as they both dug into their steaks. They might've stopped talking, but the communication was still going strong. Drake's sharp gaze followed her every move, and Mel found herself tilting her head and leaning toward him, flashing her cleavage and reveling in the way his eyes darkened. She brushed her fingers against his whenever she had the chance and let her own gaze eat him up, building one hunger as she satisfied another.

As much as she wished she'd sat next to him, so she could brush against him more freely, she was thoroughly enjoying the view of him across the table from her. He made slow economical movements, cutting his steak, chewing, swallowing. All those same things she saw people do every day took on a whole new level when he did them.

By the time Terry came to clear their plates and see if they wanted dessert, Mel was squirming in her seat.

"No, thanks," she told the waitress.

"You don't want dessert?" Drake asked after Terry had walked away.

The erotic rumble of his voice sent a stab of desire straight through Mel. She'd had enough. Her juices were flowing and she was ready for some action of the naked sort. Leaning back in her seat she met his gaze head on and went for it. "If you're on the menu, I want."

His green eyes flared bright, then darkened with a hunger that matched her own. Without a word he stood and reached for his wallet. He tossed some money down on the table, earning brownie points with the generous tip he left for Terry.

Without another word spoken he guided Melissa silently from the pub with a firm hand at the small of her back. She saw heads turn and a couple of eyebrows raise when they headed for the hotel exit instead of the street exit, and Mel knew she'd be grist for the gossip mill for a few days. It didn't bother her, though. Right then all she could think about was the electric heat between her and Drake and the delicious thrill of her thighs rubbing together as she walked.

Two minutes later she stood at Drake's side as he slid the old-fashioned key into his room door. He put his hand up in front of her, his heated gaze pinning her to the spot. "Wait," he said.

She watched as he opened the door and gave the room a quick scan. She realized he was looking for any threats or disturbances. The remembered feeling of someone having invaded her own apartment flashed in her mind, only to disappear when he turned to her and held the door open.

He raised his eyebrows and stood there, his nonverbal invitation clear. He wanted her to step into the room, but he wasn't going to guide her in. She had to enter of her own free will.

Shoulders back and hips swinging, she strolled past him and into the room. She heard the door close, and those big strong hands that had made her skin tingle all night long wrapped around her waist. He spun her around and pulled her to him. Chest to chest, thigh to thigh, his mouth landed on hers unerringly.

Melissa couldn't think, only react as Drake kissed her so passionately she practically crawled up his body in an effort to get closer. His hands ran over her body, going down her back and cupping her ass, squeezing it, his fingers digging in, making the seam of her jeans slide against the swollen folds between her legs. She arched into him, loving the feel of his hardness under her hands, the delicious ridge of his cock pressing against her belly, but hungry to be closer—to be naked with nothing between them but sweat.

Suddenly he gripped a handful of her hair and tugged her head back, exposing her neck to his ravenous mouth.

"God, yes." The moan slid from her as his teeth scraped along her jaw, leaving a blazing trail of fire. "More."

He pulled back an inch, staring down at her hungrily. "You want more?" he asked, his voice low and rough.

"Oh yes."

He let go of her and stepped back. "Then strip."

Never a shy one, she toed off her boots and reached for the snap on her jeans. She pushed the denim down her legs, taking her socks off with the pants, and then whipped her shirt off over her head. When she stood in front of him in nothing but her lace bra and flimsy thong she noticed that he'd only managed to unbutton his jeans, but nothing else.

He'd stopped to watch her.

She posed for a moment, preening under the dark fire of raw lust in his eyes. It was as if that fire went straight from his gaze into her bloodstream. Heat swept through her body, making her muscles weak and her body soften. She dropped her bra and stepped out of her underwear before planting her hands on her hips and looking him up and down, challenging him. Take me, fuck me . . . *please me*.

Drake still hadn't moved from the spot where they'd kissed, and less than a foot of space separated them. His heart pounded and his cock throbbed, almost burning with all the hot blood filling it. He'd seen better strip-teases done by women more beautiful, but he'd never felt the way he did right then.

"On the bed," he ordered.

Melissa's lips lifted in a sure smile and she moved to the bed, hips swaying, ass twitching. She crawled up on the bed and leaned back on her elbows.

"You going to give me a show now?"

He stripped off his shirt, kicked off his shoes, and shoved off his jeans, shoes, and shorts in three swift moves. "No, I'm going to give you a ride now." He walked to the edge of the bed, grabbed her ankles, and pulled her toward him.

She gasped, the sound making all the little hairs on his body stand on end. When her ass was at the edge of the bed, he wrapped her legs around his hips and bent forward, covering his mouth with his. They both moaned at the skin-on-naked-skin contact.

The rigid tips of her breasts pressed against his chest, scraping against him as she writhed beneath him. He reached between them, cupping those luscious mounds as he dragged his mouth from hers. Ripe red tips called to him and he was quick to answer, tonguing one while his fingers pinched and pulled at the other.

She arched up, her thighs tightening around his waist as her hips lifted, her wet pussy rubbing against his belly with every move. Her hands moved down and she grabbed his ass, her nails digging in as she squeezed, trying to pull him closer. "Drake," she moaned. "Fuck me."

He knew as soon as he was inside her he was going to lose it, so he bent his knees and rocked his body against hers, spreading her juices over his cock as it slid between her thick, wet folds and rubbed against her clit. He fought for control of his body and lost. The whimpers escaping from Melissa coupled with the wet warmth his cock was nudging against were too much to deny. Keeping a tight grip on the last thread of his control, Drake eased slowly into her welcoming body and fought not to come right then and there.

Christ, she felt so good! He felt so much!

Burying his face in her neck he worked to control his emotions. Melissa's body wrapped around him, fitting him better than he ever could have imagined. So perfect. Her inner muscles spasmed, the shock of it rippling over his cock and up through to his own insides. With a low groan, he lifted his head and looked into her eyes. Their gazes locked and he began to move.

She was so tight, so hot, her insides sucking at him with each stroke. Her legs gripped his hips tighter and her hands roamed over his body restlessly, scratching his back and his shoulders, sending jolts of hot raw pleasure flashing through him.

"More," she whimpered. "Harder, Drake. Fuck me, harder!"

Her nails dug hard into his shoulders as she lifted herself off the bed and nipped at his neck with sharp little teeth, shattering what little control he had.

He growled and straightened up between her legs. Gripping her hips in firm hands, he braced his knees against the mattress and fucked her hard and fast. She gasped, the sound going straight to his dick, making it swell and pulse. He slammed into her again and again, thrilling at the way her cunt clenched around him, and the ripples of sensation it sent through him.,

"Yes!" she cried out. Melissa's back arched, her breasts thrust high and her thighs tightened around his waist as her cream gushed over his cock. Sharp nails dug into his arms delivering pleasure and pain, and he came.

Thrusting deeply into her, every muscle in his body tightened and the room tilted. His whole world narrowed to the point of pleasure where their bodies met and he grunted as hot come pumped from him and filled her up.

# 6

The rasp of heavy breathing filled the room and made Melissa hyperaware of the silence. Her body was all soft and pliant, and all she wanted was to pull Drake down over her and cuddle up, but he was still as stone between her thighs. "Drake?"

He withdrew from her body and sat on the bed next to her. Silent.

Melissa lay there for a moment, basking in the pleasantly abused feel of her body. When she could muster some strength, she rolled onto her side. Reaching out a hand, she traced a finger over one of the many red scratches she'd marked his back with.

Drake shivered at her touch and she smiled. "Come here, tough guy. Lie with me."

He lay back on the bed, his head turned, concern clear in his look. "You okay? I sort of lost it there."

She smiled. "Yeah, you did. And I loved it."

The corner of his mouth turned up a little. "Yeah?"

Melissa realized he truly was concerned, and her heart thumped in her chest. "Oh yeah. In case you didn't notice I lost it a little, too."

Something flickered across his features and was gone before she could identify it. Then he smiled, the first true full smile she'd ever seen him give.

Her lover reached out and laid his hand on her trembling belly. She watched him as he moved the hand up to cup one full breast. Her nipple peaked instantly and his smile turned to a full-blown grin. "You want more?"

Her breath caught and her sex clenched. God, he was beautiful. She gazed at his big body, all hard planes and angles, his cock already swelling again and looking deliciously large.

"Yes," she said. She'd tried for firm, but her answer had been barely a breath. She cleared her throat and tried again. "Yes, I definitely want more."

Fingers skimmed over her breast to the sensitive point. He pinched and she gasped, pleasure shooting straight to her pussy. He leaned over and flicked his tongue at the other nipple, the one closest to him. Light, teasing flicks that had her arching her back and biting her lip to keep from begging.

When he finally took the whole nipple in his mouth, Melissa cried out and pressed her thighs together. He suckled, and every tug of her nipples made her pussy throb. Unable to stand it any more, she reached down and slid a stiff finger between the folds of her sex.

Drake growled, his hand leaving her other breast to move over top of hers and thrust a finger in deep. "Yes!" Their fingers slid against each other in her wet heat and she started to pant.

"Drake," she moaned.

He tore his mouth from her nipple, nibbling his way over the swollen mound of flesh and up to her neck. He thrust another finger inside her and she pulled her hand away. Her hips jerked in a wordless plea for more and he gave it to her, adding a third finger at the same time he pressed his thumb over her clit.

Melissa cried out, sensations rippling from her hungry pussy to every nerve in her body. Her movements turned frantic and she reached for Drake, pulling at his shoulders and whimpering until he moved, rolling his body on top of hers.

"Yes. Oh God, yes." She loved the feel of him, the sensation of the coarse hair on his body rubbing against her sensitive skin, the weight of him on top of her, inside her.

She reached between them and encircled his cock. It was big, so big and hard and hot in her hand, throbbing to the rapid beat of his heart. She squeezed, she stroked, she ran her thumb over the slick head and felt the vibration of Drake's groan against her neck.

His fingers thrust deeper, curling inside of her and hitting a sensitive spot. Her body bowed, her mouth opening in a soundless scream as pleasure ripped through her body. Before she could recover, Drake moved his hand and thrust his cock into her still-spasming cunt.

"Again," he commanded. "Come for me again."

He rolled his hips and ground against her, the root of his cock hitting her supersensitive clit, and her body shuddered again.

She rode a never-ending wave of pure sensation as Drake moved, playing her body like a master magician until his own guttural cry echoed through the room.

Drake kissed her neck softly. Then her ear, her jaw, and finally her lips. They shared a slow sensuous mating of tongues that melted Mel's last brain cell. When he pulled away and slid to the bed next to her she just lay there, a mindless puddle. She couldn't even open her eyes when the bed shifted and cool air flowed over her damp skin.

Time stood still as she listened to her heartbeat slow down.

Then she was lifted, and resettled in the middle of the bed, her head on a fluffy pillow, a soft blanket covered her, and then Drake's arms were around her again.

She struggled to open her eyes. "Hey," she whispered.

"Hey, yourself," he replied. His lips brushed over hers tenderly, lingering for a long moment. "Go to sleep, baby."

Warm masculine hands turned her body, pulling her to him spoon style. His breath whispered overhead and warmth surrounded her, carrying her off into a deep peaceful sleep.

Drake lay with his arms wrapped around Melissa. He'd passed out as soon as she'd settled back into his arms, but he hadn't stayed out for long. Soon his mind was prodding him awake, the need to dissect what had happened too strong to resist.

The female in his arms had made his head spin from the moment he'd first set eyes on her. Melissa stirred more than lust within him, though. Tenderness had stolen his breath, and the need to please had driven him. He'd felt every emotion with a keen sharpness that shook him to his core.

He'd never felt his own needs so sharply. Ever.

Shit. If he was honest with himself he hadn't truly felt *anything* in a long while. A very long while. And he liked it that way. Emotions were a weakness in his line of work. It was bad enough he had to sense others' feelings, but to have his own was something he couldn't allow.

# 7

Gina snapped upright in her bed, heart pounding from the images that were still flashing through her mind. She reached out a hand and felt the comforting presence of her husband at her side. Caleb Mann had no psychic talent at all, but their connection went so deep he seemed to feel her distress, even in his sleep. He rolled over and reached for her. Leaning down she pressed a soft kiss to his stubbled cheek.

"Sleep, my love," she whispered. "I'm fine."

When he snuggled back into his pillow she slid from their bed and pulled one of Caleb's sweatshirts on over her sleep shirt and shorts. The sweatshirt hung past her hips and his lingering scent calmed her a little as she made her way from their bedroom.

The red neon lights on the clock had said five-thirty, and she hoped she could talk to Angelo before Caleb woke up. Normally he'd be up with the coffee on by now, but they were on holiday, and she'd gotten him in the habit of sleeping in. The small house was still quiet and she didn't bother to turn on any lights; she just made her way to the sofa to wait.

Panic still had her heart pounding in her chest as Gina sat down, pulling her knees up and tugging the sweatshirt over them to stay warm. After a couple of deep breaths she reached for the phone and dialed from memory.

The phone rang on the other end, and rang, and rang. When the ringing stopped, all she got was voice mail, so she left a curt message. "Call me."

The birthmark on her wrist throbbed and she dialed again, another number this time, before Angelo felt her fear in his matching birthmark and called her to see what was wrong.

The phone rang on the other end and was picked up almost instantly. "Hello?"

"Hi, Jewel," she said quietly. "Is Angel there?"

"Devil, it's Gina."

Jewel hadn't spoken into the phone, but Gina had heard her easily. If she hadn't been so scared, she'd have laughed at the reminder that she was still the only person who shortened his first name and called him Angel instead of his last name. Devlin to Devil made more sense considering the life he lead, but he'd always be her Angel, no matter how many big bad things he killed.

Angelo's voice, full of worry, came over the phone line clean and clear. "What is it?"

She answered her big brother's question with one of her own. "Where's Drake?"

"He needed to get away from everyone for a while. Recharge his mental batteries and rebuild his psychic walls."

"There's more to it than that, isn't there?"

Angelo paused. Their matching birthmarks acted almost like a telepathic link between the two siblings, and his inner conflict was coming through their link loud and clear.

All he'd ever wanted to do was protect her, and it went

against everything he believed in to share the dangerous parts of his life with her. Gina gave him a minute to wrestle with his conscience knowing he would give in to her demand because they both understood her own gift was something that couldn't be ignored.

He blew out a resigned breath, then spoke quickly. "We found a lead on a pureblood shape-shifter so Drake went to check it out. A little recon, nothing more than that."

Shape-shifter.

Gina's heart kicked in her chest and she let her head fall back against the sofa. "He's in trouble, Angel."

"What did you see?"

She shook her head. All her life she'd had prophetic dreams, and sometimes they just didn't make any sense. "I don't know exactly. I saw Drake. It was dark and he was beat up and hurting, but I couldn't see where he was, or even how badly hurt he was. It was just a kaleidoscope of fear, anger, and pain."

"It's okay." The confidence in Angelo's voice eased some of her anxiety. He believed her. He always believed her, and he knew how to help her. "Take a deep breath, Gina, and close your eyes. Think back, try and see more. Is he inside or outside?"

She took a deep breath, concentrating on letting go and opening her mind. "Inside, I think."

"Is he alone?"

"No."

"Do you know the person he's with?"

She strained, trying to shift the image in her mind's eye. She could sense someone with Drake, but she couldn't see anyone. Everything around him was blurry. "I can't see," she muttered, frustration building.

"You can't see because you're scared," Angelo said. "It's okay,

Gina. It was a dream, nothing's happened yet. Drake is fine right now. Just look deeper and we'll protect him from what's to come."

Her stomach clenched and she rocked against the back of the sofa, trying to see more. She sensed Caleb next to her before his hand touched her shoulder and he eased down beside her.

"Shhh," he crooned. His arm went around her and he pulled her against his side, his lips brushing against her ear as he spoke softly. "I'm here, sweetheart. Relax and breathe deep. You can do this. You can do anything."

The tightness in Gina's chest eased. Caleb had become her rock, grounding her with his love. With him at her side she *could* do anything.

Without opening her eyes she relaxed against his warm body and let her head fall against his shoulder. She breathed deep, concentrating on the image in her mind of the man who was like another brother to her. Her pulse slowed and she sank deeper into her own subconscious.

The fog in her vision cleared and she gasped. Her eyes popped open and she stared at Caleb. "He's in some sort of hospital facility," she said into the phone.

"Who else did you see? You said he wasn't alone."

"I didn't see anyone else, but I can *feel* that someone else is there."

A chill went through her and she met her husband's gaze. "Call him. Warn him. It hasn't happened yet, Angelo. Tell Drake to come home before he finds that shape-shifter. It's going to kill him!"

"I will, Gina. It's okay, it's all going to be okay. Just hold on a minute, I'll get him on his cell right now."

Gina buried her head in her husband's shoulder as she listened to Angelo on the other end. She fought to control the fear rushing through her. She knew it stemmed from the fact that a wild animal had killed her father. A wolf she still believed was a werewolf, even though Angelo refused to confirm her suspicions.

"Wheeler." Angelo's voice carried easily to Gina. "What do you know so far?"

She listened while Angelo explained her dream to Drake, the tension around her heart easing but not disappearing. By the time he hung up with Drake, then reassured her again, she'd made her decision.

Gina hung up the phone and faced Caleb. She was not going to lose another family member.

The call from Devil had dragged him from the bundle of warm, willing woman in his arms way too early. If it had been anyone other than his partner calling he'd have let it ring and gone for another round with Melissa before confronting her with the whole shape-shifter thing. But the distinctive ring tone of "*The Devil Went Down To Georgia*" ensured he couldn't ignore the call.

Devil would call only if it were important, and Gina having a dream like the one he'd just described was important.

He flipped the phone closed and thought about the dream. Gina's premonitions were good as gold. Something was about to go down.

A soft knock at the hotel room door interrupted his thoughts.

The knock came again, firmer and louder this time, and he left the bathroom, the distressing sadness coming from the other side of the door calling to him.

Melissa was half out of the bed when Drake emerged from the bathroom, completely naked with his cell phone in hand. A wave of desire washed over him at the sight of her sleepy eyes and swollen lips, and he bit back a groan. He was nowhere near done with that female.

He waved a hand at her in a "stay there" motion and pulled on a pair of boxer shorts quickly before going to the door. The urgency of the person on the other side came through loud and clear. Without hesitation he pulled the door open, surprised to see their waitress from the night before standing there.

He pulled her into the room. "What happened?"

The pretty blonde ignored him and stared at Melissa, who was back under the covers.

"Mel," she said, wringing her hands in front of her. "Something bad has happened."

# 8

Time stood still as Melissa ran down Main Street toward her bookstore in nothing more than her boots, jeans, and shirt. Everything seemed to be in slow motion, except her heartbeat. It pounded in her chest, her pulse racing as she fought to suck air into her lungs. "It's not true, it's not true."

The mantra repeating over and over in her head was the only thing that kept her moving. She could see the ambulance and the RCMP car in front of her building, and she picked up her pace. She had to see for herself. Constable John Cane tried to stop her when she reached the store.

"Mel, stop." His hands reached for her but she dodged him easily. "Melissa!"

She ran up the back stairs and stopped dead inside her apartment. Her wooden coffee table was in pieces, the sofa was turned over, and broken glass littered the floor. And in the middle of the room, sprawled out on the floor was her best friend.

Everything came alive again. The blood on the floor so vibrant it hurt her eyes. The sound of the paramedics packing up, the squawk of the police radio drowning out her own thoughts.

"No," she muttered, racing into the room. She dropped to her knees beside the bloody and broken body and reached for her friend, only to be grabbed from behind and pulled back.

"Erin, no. You're okay, Erin," she cried out, struggling against the bands of steel wrapped around her. She needed to get to Erin! "Stop playing. This isn't funny!"

She stared at her best friend's bruised pixie face, waiting for the devilish smile to emerge. Waiting for the glassy eyes to blink. "Blink, damn you!" she yelled. "Blink!"

Silence descended on the room and John stepped into her line of vision, reaching out as if to touch her, only to be stopped by the low growl that came from behind her. Melissa realized it was Drake holding her, and everything Terry had told her was true. Everything she saw was *real*.

Her knees collapsed beneath her.

Erin was dead.

Drake swept Melissa up into his arms and carried her from the apartment. Her mind floated for a few minutes as grief took over. Her childhood accomplice, her partner in all things fun, her best friend . . . was dead.

She'd let her down. Erin had always been there for her, through her first change, through her first heartbreak, through her grandmother's death. Erin had always had her back. And Mel hadn't been there when Erin had needed her most. Now she'd never see Erin smile again. Never fight with her, and never laugh with her again.

A low keening cry came from deep inside her soul and she started to shake. Warm hands cupped her head, tilting it back so that she was staring into compelling emerald-green eyes.

"Open up for me, baby." His deep voice was hypnotic, reaching past the fog in her mind and making her aware of the pressure pushing at her mind. "Let me in, Melissa. I can help you."

Let him in? Help her? How about help Erin? Could he help her?

"C'mon, Melissa." He pleaded with her. "Let me in."

Unable to resist, she lifted a hand and touched his cheek. The pressure in her head swelled then burst through her psychic shields. Inexplicable warmth swept through her, washing away the worst of her fear and heartbreak.

It was like coming awake from a dream—a true nightmare. She became aware of the blanket wrapped around her, and dampness on her cheeks from tears she'd unknowingly shed. She also realized that the last member of her family was gone. Forever.

Anger, swift and sure, fired up her blood and she pulled away from Drake. Jumping up from his lap, she strode away from the police cruiser he'd sat in and planted herself in front of John Cane. "Tell me what happened."

Drake forced himself to stand back and let Melissa question the RCMP officer. His chest ached with the need to snatch her up and take her away from the crime scene. He wanted to soothe her, to make her forget what she'd just seen, even if it was only for a short while. But it didn't matter what he wanted, not right then. Right then Melissa needed answers and he was going to help her get them, even if it meant standing back and doing nothing.

Constable John Cane was a lean guy who looked to be in his late thirties. A little bit of gray at his temples and a tiredness to his features told Drake this wasn't the cop's first murder scene. The tight edge to his jawline and his watchful gaze told him that the cop was no easy mark. Melissa wasn't intimidated, though. She pulled the blanket closer around her shoulders and stood her ground in front of the weary cop.

Admiration for her ran through Drake at her straight spine

and unwavering voice as she demanded answers. "Don't hold back with me either, John. I want to know everything."

"It looks like she interrupted a robbery in progress. Where were you this morning, Mel? Do you know why she was there?"

"A robbery?" Her voice hit a high note, and Drake had to fight the urge to step forward and touch her. He didn't need his powers to know she was hurting. "C'mon, John, when was the last time there was a robbery in Chadwick?"

"There were signs that the intruder had been in the store before going upstairs to the apartment."

"What signs?"

Cane grimaced. "The cash register was empty and back door unlocked."

"I'm not an idiot. I don't leave cash in the drawer at night. There's no reason for anyone to break into my store, or my apartment."

"It's the middle of winter, Mel. We might not be in the middle of a metropolitan city, but there are still a few homeless around here. Maybe one of them missed the curfew at the shelter and needed someplace warm to sleep."

"You think a homeless person beat the crap out of Erin? That's bullshit, and you know it."

"Mel . . ."

"Erin knew how to fight, John. Her dad taught us both karate from the time we were children, and we've kept it up." Melissa stepped forward, pointing a finger in the cop's face. "Whoever did that to her, it was someone who knew what they were doing."

Drake put his hands on her shoulders and pulled her back until she leaned against his chest. He wasn't holding her so much as letting her know she wasn't alone and lending her some support.

"You never told me why she would be knocking on your door at six in the morning, Mel."

"She probably wanted to go for an early morning hike. She's been super-restless what with Troy not home for—Troy. Oh God, Troy. Does he know? Has anyone contacted him?"

The cop assured her they'd sent someone to talk to Troy's parents, who would then track down their son. "Where were you this morning, Mel? Why weren't you home?"

Her back stiffened, and before she could say anything Drake spoke up. "She was with me." He reached around her and held his hand out to the cop. "Drake Wheeler."

They clasped hands and Drake sensed the man's turmoil. He'd liked Erin. He liked Melissa, too. But he was suspicious.

"You new in town, Wheeler?"

"Just visiting for the holidays."

The cops eyes jumped from him to Melissa. "And you were together all night . . . and this morning?"

"That's right," she said.

"I see." His features tightened and there was a moment of heavy silence before he continued. "I'm afraid that's all we can tell you right now, Mel. I'll contact you when we know more."

It was a clear dismissal, and Melissa took it in silence. Spinning on her heel she strode away from them, only to stop abruptly ten feet away. Drake stared at her rigid posture for a moment before turning back to the RCMP officer.

He reached for his wallet before turning to Cane. "Melissa will be with me. The number for my cell phone is on here. Use it anytime, day or night." Drake handed him a business card, ignoring the surprise on the man's face, then went to stand in front of Melissa.

Melissa stood shivering in the middle of the sidewalk. The town was waking up, despite the fact that it was still dark out.

Winter made for long nights in the mountains, but that didn't mean people didn't go on.

Her breath caught in her throat. How could she go on? The bookstore building was crawling with people in uniforms, doing their job as they kept a wary eye on her. She could feel the eyes of the townspeople on her, too, as they peered out from the warm safety of their own homes, but no one came to see her. Even Terry had stayed back at the hotel when Melissa had run off.

Erin had been all she'd had. She had no one left now.

She was all alone.

A warm body brushed against her arm, and then Drake stood in front of her. "Why don't you come back to the hotel with me?" he asked.

"Why?"

"You can't stay here," he said simply.

*And I have nowhere else to go*, she thought.

Pain turned to anger and she lashed out, "And you think I should go with you? You think you know me? That just because we fucked, you're my friend?"

His eyes blazed brightly for a brief moment. His chest rose and fell as he sucked in a deep breath. He stepped forward, his voice low and calm as he spoke. "No, I don't think we're friends, and I might not know *you*, but I do know *what* you are. And we both know there is more to this situation than what's on the surface."

Stunned, she stared at him. Then her heart jumped and her brain kick-started. She wanted to deny it. She wanted to tell him she didn't know what the hell he was talking about, but the clear knowledge in his gaze told her arguing would be hopeless. This was the last thing she needed just now.

Drake knew her secret.

"Let's go," she said with a sharp nod.

# 9

Richard Bradley watched the couple from his car. It was early yet, with the sky just starting to lighten behind the mountains, but he could see them clearly. He was parked a block up the road, in front of small clapboard house that looked empty for the holidays. He'd parked there with his hand twitching on the laptop as he watched the police arrive, the ambulance arrive, and finally Melissa Montrose arrived.

He hadn't expected the man who'd arrived with her.

The big guy could be trouble. He had the look of a cop or a soldier, and he was protective as hell of the woman. Even from a block away, without hearing anything said, he could see that.

Shit. This was not going as smoothly as he'd hoped. The little redhead had caught him by surprise in Montrose's apartment before he'd had a chance to find the confirmation he'd been looking for. He didn't like killing humans—it would draw attention to what he was doing and make it harder to get to his prey. But eliminating the redhead had been a must . . . and it hadn't been as easy as it should've been.

He pulled a small plastic bottle from his coat pocket, popped the top off, and swallowed the painkillers dry. She'd put up a good fight, but in the end she'd been no match for him.

The big blond might be, though, and it was starting to look like Bradley would have to go through him to get to Montrose.

# 10

---

Melissa walked past Drake and into the middle of his hotel room. Her body ached and her limbs were heavy, but not as heavy as her heart. She shouldn't be in this hotel room. What did she know about Drake Wheeler? Nothing other than his name and the fact that he was an intense lover.

He was intense, period.

She should be afraid. An intense stranger who knew her secret walks into her life one day, and the next her best friend is dead, murdered in her apartment. Melissa remembered the book he'd bought from her the day before, and pain throbbed in her chest. Should she have seen this coming?

Turning to face Drake, she forced the words past her lips. "Did you have anything to do with this?"

"I was with you all night."

"That doesn't answer my question."

"No." Drake stepped closer, his gaze never wavering. "I had nothing to do with Erin getting killed."

She folded her arms across her chest and nodded at the book

on the desk. "But you came here on a hunt, didn't you? For me."

He shook his head. "I came to Chadwick hoping to find a shape-shifter, but it wasn't a *hunt*. I'm not here to hurt you, I didn't break into your apartment at any point in time, and I didn't kill Erin."

"But you've hunted before, killed before."

He didn't flinch. "Yes."

Numb, she turned away from him and collapsed onto the unmade bed. She didn't even care anymore. Erin was gone, what did it matter?

Drake saw Melissa crumple and couldn't hold back any longer. Moving swiftly he sat at the top of the bed and leaned back against the headboard. He reached out and lifted Melissa, rearranging her on the bed between his legs. Bending his knees he wrapped his arms around her and cushioned her with his body.

"No," she muttered, twisting and tugging, trying to get away from him. Instinct told him she wasn't really fighting him but what she was feeling. She was fighting the reality of Erin's death and the pain that it caused.

He held tight to her squirming body, aching deep inside as her tears started to flow. These weren't the same tears of shock and anger she'd shed at the bookstore; these were tears of loss. Of grief.

The tears turned to sobs and she fell back against his chest, curling into him when she couldn't fight herself any longer. Her tears ripped at his insides, clawing at him in way that he couldn't combat. It felt as if someone had slammed a baseball bat into his gut and he struggled to breathe. He wanted to take the pain away, to make her smile and laugh and know that life would go on. But he couldn't do that. The grief process was a natural one that even he couldn't fuck with.

He didn't have the words to make her feel better, but he could hold her. And when she ran out of tears, he would show her that there was still a reason to go on.

Melissa cried herself to sleep in Drake's arms. His room had a big window with an eastern view and he watched the sun peek over the mountain from his position on the bed. So much had happened in just a couple of short days, and yet he knew it was just the beginning.

Not being able to read Melissa, Gina's premonition, and Erin's death all pointed to something bigger than just finding a shape-shifter. He refused to think of Melissa as a skinwalker. Not after all he'd heard from Jewel and what he'd gleaned from the book he'd bought the day before. He might not be able to sense her emotions, but he knew she wasn't evil.

Melissa shifted in his arms, her legs stretching out as a heavy sigh puffed from her parted lips. She was emotionally exhausted and in a deep sleep. He wanted to stay there with her in his arms, but he had things to do. Things he needed to do before she woke up.

After easing out from behind her, he filled the space with pillows and watched as she snuggled against them. He slid her boots off her feet and pulled a blanket up around her shoulders, tucking her in before brushing a kiss over her tearstained cheek. His legs had cramped up long ago, but the pins and needles each movement caused were a small price to pay to offer comfort.

Moving to the far side of the room, he pulled his cell phone from his pocket and dialed his partner.

"Found her," he said when Devil answered.

"Is she willing to come in and met with Nadya? Is she someone we *want* to meet with her?"

"I think she'll be great with the kid, but things are starting to happen here, and I'm not sure when I'll be able to bring her in."

The tension in Devil's voice spiked. "What things?"

Drake told him about the break-in and the murder.

"And she was with you when this happened?" Devil asked after a pause. "Are you thinking with your dick, Wheeler?"

Ignoring the flare of anger at his partner's judgment, Drake went on. "Gina's dream means there's more trouble to come, and I'm not ready to leave this woman behind to deal with this on her own."

They talked for another minute. Devil had been checking out Melissa Montrose after their phone call earlier that morning, but so far, nothing had popped. The woman was a shifter, but she'd kept under the radar in every way they could find.

He hung up with Devil, and then he called Nadya.

"Hey, squirt," he said when she answered. Never one to talk unnecessarily, he got straight to the point. "I found a shapeshifter for you."

"No shit!"

He laughed. "No shit."

"Is it a guy? A girl? Please don't tell me it's some smelly old man who lives in a freak'n cave somewhere."

Drake bit back a laugh. The girl had imagination. "She's a pretty young lady who lives in a normal apartment and works a normal job."

"Do I get to meet her? I want to meet her, Drake. No more of this working from books and legends shit. It's like I'm never out of school. I want to meet her, and talk to her, and—"

"Slow down," he cautioned. He didn't know anything about kids, but he knew Nadya, and the excitement and relief in her voice told him he'd done the right thing in looking for one of her own kind. Being a teenager was tough enough; being a teenager with uncontrollable magick was bound to be over-whelming. "I haven't actually told her about you yet. There's some other stuff we need to deal with first."

"What other stuff? I thought you were just on a retreat or something."

"It was a work holiday." He went on to assure her that he was sure Melissa would go to Vancouver and hang out with her for a while before saying good-bye. "I just wanted to let you know you're not alone, brat."

There was a minute of silence on the phone. "Nadya?"

"Thank you," she said softly.

"You're welcome. I've got to go now; I'll see you in a few days."

He hung up the phone and stared at the sleeping female on the bed. Before he'd met her, other people's emotions were pretty much all he felt. Now the tightness in his chest told him something was shifting, and he wasn't sure it was a good thing.

Melissa opened her eyes, shocked to see sunlight streaming in the hotel room window. It was December, and Chadwick was deep in a valley of the Selkirk Mountains, which meant the sun didn't shine down on the town until at least eight o'clock. The hotel room?

Everything came rushing back to her at once, and she squeezed her eyes shut.

"Melissa?"

She didn't want to move, didn't want to answer. She just wanted to go back to sleep and hope it was all a bad dream. But she couldn't. But she wasn't ready to deal with Drake just yet, either.

A glance at the bedside clock showed it was almost noon. She rolled from the bed in one quick movement, and passed him on her way to the bathroom. "I need to take a shower," she said.

With a sharp twist of her wrists she turned on the shower and stepped back. She stripped off her clothes, the same clothes she'd put on for her dinner date with the man in the other room. She didn't bother waiting for the water temperature to level out, she just pushed aside the pretty green fabric shower curtain and stepped into the tub.

Warm water plastered her hair to her scalp and she stood there, letting the water wash away the hot tears that streamed silently down her cheeks. Erin—pretty, baby-faced Erin who'd finally made the decision to move on from the dead-end relationship that had kept her from true happiness for too long—was gone.

Mel lost track of time as she stood under the steady spray of pressurized water. Memories flowed through her mind like movies. The two of them in pigtails and white Karate Gei's wrestling around on the mat. Erin's first attempt at wearing makeup. Erin holding Mel as she cried because Mel's dad was gone and nobody knew what had happened to him. Their first double date. Erin bathing her face with a cool washcloth when the full moon had gifted her with her powers. Mel holding Erin when the search and rescue failed to find her parents in time. The two of them holding hands as they walked away from Mel's grandmother's funeral. The movie stalled with the sight of Erin's unblinking eyes as she lay on the floor of Mel's apartment.

Gentle hands cupped Mel's shoulders and pulled her back against a hard chest. Without thinking Mel turned and pulled Drake's head down to hers. She needed this, she needed him. Now.

She kissed him with a fervent hunger, using the passion he stirred so easily to push past the pain. She speared her tongue between his lips and demand his ardent response. Her hands clutched at his shoulders, holding him, pulling him closer as she lifted a leg and hooked it over his hip.

As if he knew exactly what she wanted, what she *needed*, he took control. He turned them until her back was against the cool tile wall and pressed his full length against her. The hard rod of his erection was hot against her belly, telling her he wanted her as much as she wanted him, but he didn't rush things. One hand cupped her cheek, and his lips gentled.

He loved her slowly and thoroughly. His lips soft, his hands touching, teasing, and slowly bringing life back to her mind and her heart. He cupped her breasts, his mouth traveling, teeth scraping along her neck and down until he sucked a hard nipple into his mouth. He went from one to the other as one hand slid between their bodies and skimmed over her belly.

She whimpered when he brushed against her core, and sighed when he thrust two fingers deep. The heel of his hand rubbed against her clit, and his fingers massaged her inner walls, setting her system afire.

"That's it," Drake murmured as he straightened up and looked down at her. "Let go, baby. Enjoy the ride."

His fingers curved and her nails dug into his shoulders as pleasure was torn from her core and spread throughout her body and soul.

When her orgasm faded Drake's cock was sliding between her slick pussy lips and into her body. She pressed her face into the crook of his neck and sucked his clean manly scent into her lungs as he began to move.

She felt every inch of his slow thrusts as languorous pleasure pooled low in her belly and began to spread until her whole body trembled and a gentle orgasm washed away the last of her tears.

"Yes," Drake said on a sigh. He thrust one final time, deep and true, and his body shuddered in her arms.

He stepped back and cupped her cheek with his hand. "Hey," he said. "You okay?"

Mel opened her eyes and gazed at the man who'd used his body to remind her that she was still alive. His craggy features were soft, and concern filled his intense gaze. She gave him a small smile. "Yeah," she whispered. "I'm okay."

Not great, but better.

She ushered him from the shower with a light pat on his firm ass.

"I just need to clean up. I'll be right out." She met his eyes. "We need to talk."

Melissa took the time she used to wash to think about what she was about to do. Her family was gone, but others of her kind still depended on her. Her mind didn't want to accept that Erin was dead just because she'd been her friend, but her instincts told her that was so. The bookstore break-in could've just been a random thing, but not her apartment. Someone had deliberately gone upstairs for something, and Erin had found them.

If Melissa had been at home, instead of with Drake, Erin would still be alive. A part of her wanted to blame Drake, but she was too smart for that. It was her fault, and her doing. But he was going to help her settle the score.

Determination filled her heart and her mind, strengthening her soul.

She could hunt in the wild, shifting into a predator and stalking small prey was nothing new to her. But small prey wasn't what she wanted now, and she didn't think she'd find Erin's killer in the forest.

## 11

Melissa strode into the room with a towel wrapped around her body, and Drake's dick twitched. Her skin looked all soft and smooth, and a stray water droplet trailed down her collarbone and into the valley of her breasts, making him want to lick her all over.

*Calm the fuck down*, he told himself.

"There's a T-shirt and a pair of boxer shorts for you to wear." He nodded toward the bed. "If you bring your clothes out we can send them to the hotel laundry while we eat."

"Sounds good," she said, and dropped the towel.

If he were anything resembling a gentleman he would've turned his back and let her dress with a modicum of privacy, but he wasn't. Instead, Drake tortured himself by leaning against the small work desk and watching her every move.

Hot blood flowed through him and settled low in his groin, but his physical reaction to her wasn't surprising. What surprised him was the wave of tenderness that tempered his arousal.

Turning away, he pulled out his cell phone and pretended to check his text messages, all the while struggling to get a grip on his emotions. *His* emotions! Three days ago he'd barely been able to feel sexual pleasure without dropping his shields and riding the wave of his partner's satisfaction and here he was fighting to control his need to nurture, protect, and please a woman he barely knew.

Enough already. Now was not the time to be weak. Now was the time to be smart.

Closing up his phone he turned to the woman sitting cross-legged in the middle of his bed. His big, unmade bed that still smelled of sex. Unbelievable, mind-altering, headboard-banging sex that he was more than ready to have another round of.

*Focus, damn it!* He'd never been so randy in his life. Even as a teenager he'd had *some* control over his libido.

Drake tore his gaze from the mussed sheets and checked Melissa out. He didn't need to be able to read her to see the change that had come over her. Gone was the sultry and flirta-tious woman who'd challenged him to get on her good side. The vulnerable lover with a broken heart from less than an hour ago was also nowhere to be seen. In front of him sat a woman with a spine of steel, forged in pain and grief—a woman who'd shut herself off.

Understanding the need to protect one's self, Drake kept his mouth shut and concentrated on the task ahead. As an empath, it was his natural inclination to want to heal, and right then the only way he could help Melissa heal was to help her find out the truth about what happened in her apartment.

"Let's start with, why would someone be after you?" he said softly.

She shrugged. "My kind has always been hunted. Why were you after me?"

"I wasn't after *you*, Melissa. I was hoping to find a pure-blood shape-shifter though."

"Why? And even better, how did you find me?"

He wasn't ready to tell her about Nadya just yet so he skipped over the why of things and went to the how. "A while ago I was sent out to take down a werewolf that was killing humans. I found some papers in his house that pointed to a skinwalker being in Chadwick."

"So you are a hunter."

"Of a sort." She shivered at his confirmation, and Drake fought the desire to reach out to her. "I didn't lie, Melissa. I work for a private security company that has many specialties, one of which is hunting and killing the things that hunt humans."

"I'm *not* a skinwalker. I don't hunt humans; I've never killed anything bigger than a rabbit in my life!"

"I know. And your name isn't Sharza either, but I still think you're who the werewolf was trying to find."

Something flashed in her dark eyes and his internal radar sounded. "What?" he asked when she remained quiet.

She raised an eyebrow at him. "What, what?"

He folded his arms across his chest and stared at her. "You want to play games or you want to be straight with me?"

Melissa thought about it. She'd known Drake less than forty-eight hours. She had no real reason to trust him, but she needed him, so she'd be straight with him. To a point.

"What did he have that mentioned the Sharza?"

One blond eyebrow lifted. "*The* Sharza?" he asked.

Mel nodded, her heart pounding in her chest.

Drake shook his head. "Nothing much, just the word. We assumed it was a name. I'm guessing now we were wrong?"

"Who's we?"

She could see that his patience was starting to wear thin, but he answered her anyway. "My partner, Angelo Devlin, and his girlfriend, Jewel Kattalis." He nodded at her. "Your turn now. What's the Sharza?"

Mel looked at him, telling him this went against every rule she'd been raised to follow. It could potentially be the straw that wiped out her entire race, yet she had no one else to turn to. She needed to tell someone about the lines, the book, the database, even if only because something might happen to her.

"You were partly right. The Sharza is a person . . . or I should say it's a *title*. The Sharza is the keeper of the lines of my people, the genealogist who keeps track of all the shape-shifter family trees. Deaths, births, and for the last century since we've spread out so much, the whereabouts."

Drake nodded, his expression thoughtful. "So this person knows where all the shape-shifters in the world are?"

"Yes."

He stared at her. "You're the Sharza, aren't you?"

She took a deep breath and nodded. "I'm the Sharza for this generation."

Drake nodded, but stayed silent.

Mel mentally threw up her hands. He'd never been exactly talkative before, so she didn't know why she'd expected this revelation to change anything. It would sure be nice to know what the guy was thinking, though.

When he did finally speak again, it wasn't a question, it was a command. "Tell me everything."

Bristling, she bit back her instinctive response to tell him where to go and told him about her race.

For the next two hours she explained that for centuries her kind had been organized, ruled by a monarchy. They'd lived together, first as tribes, then as communities separate from other races, until they couldn't any longer. They'd created settlements that had grown into towns when humans started to spread. They'd welcomed a small amount of integration but had always kept what they could do, what they were, a secret.

Then more people had come and the towns had grown into

cities and the world got smaller. Shape-shifters started to spread out and assimilate completely within the human societies.

"And the royal family?"

"The monarchy remained, but the king became less of a ruler, and more of a . . . an enforcer." Melissa smiled at him. "We all knew the rules of survival, and they were basic. Keep our secret from humans and no hunting humans."

"And when someone broke the rules?"

"They became a threat to the survival of our kind. The king, or his enforcer, usually one of his sons, would eliminate any threat to our kind." She sighed, her fingers pulling at a loose thread on the edge of the blanket. "In the early 1950s our numbers dropped dramatically, and we discovered a fanatical religious group had somehow learned of our existence, and they were hunting us."

There was a knock on the door and she jumped. Drake looked at his watch. "Room service," he told her.

He reached out and covered her fidgeting hand, his voice firm and ripe with honesty when he spoke. "I'm not part of that group. You don't have to fear me, or my friends."

Melissa watched as Drake opened the door and paid cash before wheeling a cart full of food into the room.

She'd known he wasn't dumb, but his straightforward questions and observations made Mel feel better. With him on her side, Erin's killer was definitely living on borrowed time.

"Do you think it was them . . . whoever it was that broke into your apartment? The religious group?" Drake asked after they were both seated at the desk with food in front of them.

Steak, potatoes, and veggies. Yum, Drake knew what she liked.

"Yes . . . No . . . not really." She blew out a frustrated breath. "I'm not sure what to think. As much as I want to think it was just a random break-in gone wrong, I can't quite make myself believe it. But at the same time, it's hard to believe the Soldiers of Chi-Rho have tracked me to Chadwick, or that they would kill Erin, a human."

Drake nodded, chewing thoughtfully. "How do you keep track of everyone now?" he asked after he swallowed.

She smiled. "I'm a modern girl. I set up a database and secure Web site where all the shape-shifters can keep in touch."

"So there are others out there who know who you are? Not just that you're a shape-shifter, but that you're the Sharza?"

"No." She stabbed a baby carrot with her fork. "I'm on the forums as myself, "BookGeek." People e-mail the Sharza with news, and she comes out only to make announcements."

"And the others don't question it?"

She shrugged. "How can they? The whole digital cyber thing is new, with no precedent. In our history everyone knew who the keeper of the lines was, but in history we all lived as a clan as well. We've adjusted with the times."

"Pretty smart stuff," Drake said with a small nod.

Mel ducked her head and cut another piece of steak, strangely pleased at his praise.

# 12

"Tell me again that you are not going to go on an actual hunt with your brother," Caleb said as he steered his truck through downtown Vancouver to West Hastings Street.

"I'm not going to go on a hunt with my brother," Gina repeated dutifully.

"Gina." Her name came out in a mixture of love and frustration. "This is crazy."

Gina looked over at the man behind the wheel. He was well put together with a precise haircut and clothes that never seemed to get dirty, despite the fact that he ran a construction company. Sometimes she wondered what she'd done to deserve having such a beautiful, stable, heart-strong man walk into her life. Most times she just thanked all the gods that he had. Without him, she'd be lost.

She reached over and put her hand on his leg, rubbing her thumb against the hard muscle there.

"We're not here because I want a thrill, Caleb. I promise I'll do my best not to put myself in harm's way, but I refuse to sit at home in Pearson when I know I might be able to help." She paused. "If Gabe were in trouble, you know nothing would stop you from doing whatever you needed to in order to help him."

"Low blow," he muttered as he pulled the truck into the parking lot next to one of the large glossy office buildings and found an empty spot. "I understand why we're here, but I don't have to like it."

Once the truck was turned off, he turned to Gina and giddiness fluttered in her tummy. It didn't matter that she knew him as well as he knew her, he'd always be able to give her butterflies with just a look from those true-blue eyes of his.

His gaze was so full of love and determination that her heart melted. Her man was very much a lover, but he'd fight when his loved ones were threatened. She hated that in the time they were together his world had been turned upside down, in more ways than one, but she was also selfishly glad to have him at her side.

"I won't get involved any more than is absolutely necessary," she promised.

Caleb rolled his eyes and leaned toward her. "That's something at least," he muttered before pressing his lips against her in a kiss that was way too brief. "Let's do this before I decide to find a hotel and tie you to the bed until this whole thing is over."

A shiver of desire raced through Gina at his words and she hesitated. Caleb climbed out of the truck and turned, surprised to see her still sitting there. He tilted his head and gave her a questioning look.

"I'm debating," she said with a naughty grin. "I've always wanted to try bondage."

Caleb laughed, red creeping up his neck, and Gina quickly slid across the bench seat and out of the truck. "I love you," she said, standing on tiptoe and planting a kiss on his soft lips.

"I love you, too." He smacked her on the ass, not lightly. "Now get moving before I change my mind."

They made their way to the main doors of the high-rise. She had to admit, she hadn't expected to find the Hunter Protection Group housed in such a nice building. The lobby was open and airy with a large metal sculpture in the middle that lent to the affluent business air.

Several yards in front of a large bank of elevators was a security check-in desk. A man sat behind the big marble desk and a woman stood in front of it. Both wore average business attire, if expensive looking, and both wore pleasant expressions. Yet the vibe coming off them was pure "Don't fuck with me."

That was fine; Gina wasn't in the mood to be fucked with either.

She stepped up to the desk, noting that the marble hid what looked to be the dashboard of a spaceship full of video screens, buttons, and dials, and she asked what floor the Hunter Protection Group was on.

"Who would you like to see, ma'am?"

"Angelo Devlin, please."

"I'll just call up and see if he's available," he said smoothly as he reached for the black handset built into the desk's console.

A tingle of unease rippled through her. "That's not necessary," she said. "Just tell me where his office is and we'll go straight there."

Angel was going to have a fit when he found out she was there. She'd really prefer it be in private and not in the ritzy lobby.

The guard ignored her and spoke into the phone. He pushed a button and she saw her photo flash onto the dashboard screen. Shit. She looked straight ahead and waved into the camera.

The guard hung up the phone and smiled at her. "He'll be right down to escort you upstairs, ma'am."

"Are you ready for this?" Caleb whispered in her ear.

"I can handle my brother," she said.

His lips twitched and he looked over her shoulder. "Uh-huh."

She turned to see her older brother stalking toward them, tension clear in every line of his hard body.

Angelo Devlin was tall, dark, and handsome . . . and pissed off. Despite that, he wrapped his arms around her and hugged her tight the instant she was within reach. He held onto her for a long minute, then set her down and shook hands with Caleb.

"What the hell are you two doing here?" he asked in a deceptively soft voice.

"You invited us for Christmas."

"Christmas is more than week away, Gina."

"You know why we're here, Angel." There was no need to pretend with her brother. "Drake is in trouble, and I can help."

She saw the struggle in his eyes. He knew she could help, he believed in her and her gift, but he also had a protective streak wider than the Grand Canyon.

Finally he sighed and she knew she'd won. For now.

# 13

"I need to get into my apartment."

They'd been sitting in silence for almost an hour, each with their own thoughts as they ate the late lunch room service had delivered.

He shouldn't have been surprised that her thoughts had been along a similar line to his own.

"I've noticed this town rolls up the sidewalks at ten o'clock. We'll go after midnight."

"We should go right now."

He shook his head. "It's been less than twenty-four hours. Your apartment, and most likely the bookstore, too, is still a crime scene. Technically, we'll have to break into your place."

She muttered something he didn't catch and he bit back a smile. Impatient and angry was better than grief-stricken and crying.

Drake stood, reaching for his jacket as he moved toward the door.

Melissa stared at him. "Where are you going?"

He took in her bouncing knee and the way her gaze kept darting to the door, and he tensed. Melissa was going stir-crazy.

"I'm going for a walk around town. I want to see what people are saying." And *feeling*.

She jumped from the bed. "Wait! I'm coming with you."

"No. It's best if I go alone."

"No way! You're a stranger in this town. People won't tell you anything."

Damn it! He'd known this was going to happen.

Bracing himself for an argument, he turned to Melissa. "It's *because* I'm a stranger that I'll learn more alone than I would if you were with me. I don't need them to talk to me. They'll ignore me and talk to each other. If you're with me they'll get all solicitous and comforting and they won't do that freely."

She scowled. "That's stupid. I've lost my dad and my grandmother, and the people here have always been supportive."

He squelched the sympathy stirring inside him and stared her down.

"Were your dad and your grandmother murdered in your apartment while you spent the night in a stranger's hotel room?"

Her eyes rounded and her face went white, then her temper sparked and color flooded her cheeks. "You bastard!"

"This is an unusual situation, you know that, Melissa. We have no idea who, why, or what for that matter, killed Erin. I know you want answers to those questions, but you're going to have to trust me to help you get them." He gave her a deliberate look up and down her body. "Besides, you can't go around town wearing a T-shirt and boxer shorts."

Before he could change his mind, Drake left.

Melissa fumed silently as she paced barefoot on the plush Berber carpet. She'd planned to get dressed and go find out what was going on in spite of Drake's insistence that he'd learn nothing if she were with him, but then her clothes had arrived.

The clothes were fine, but Jay, the delivery guy who was an aspiring author and who'd spent many an afternoon in the bookstore talking plot and characters with her, hadn't been able to look her in the eye.

He'd handed her the clothes and refused her tip, then mumbled, "Sorry to hear about Erin," before turning and hightailing it down the hallway.

It hurt that someone she knew would snub her at a time like this, and it pissed her off that Drake had been right. Judging by Jay's actions, the residents of Chadwick wouldn't speak freely about what happened to Erin with her around.

What pissed her off even more was that, in the short time since Drake had gone, she'd realized that he hadn't really answered any of *her* questions during their little talk.

Sure, he'd told her how he found her, sort of, but not why. And that was a question mark that hung heavy on her mind. She'd trusted him with her secret, and he'd told her next to nothing.

For all she knew he wasn't going to share anything he learned on this little sojourn around town either. Temper heated her blood and she ground her teeth. Who made him boss? She ran her own business, the sole owner, in fact, as well as looking after herself ever since the death of her grandmother.

Screw it. If he wasn't going to answer her questions, she'd find her own answers.

Stalking over to the window, she opened it up, stepped back from it, and stripped off her clothes. Then with a thought, she shifted, and flew out the window.

The bookstore was Drake's first stop, and sure enough, it was sealed up with crime scene tape. The good news was that there was no one else there. No techs or investigators hanging around. He spun on his heel and walked to the other end of Main Street where the four-way intersection led to the highway exit out of town. He passed the intersection and walked past a lumberyard and found what he'd been looking for on the very edge of town.

The nondescript brick structure had a red and white flag mounted on one corner of the building and a red, white, and blue one with a big yellow setting sun on the other. The Canadian flag and the provincial flag both flapped in the wind, helping the utilitarian building fit into the picturesque scenery.

Drake pulled open the glass door bearing the shield with maple leaves, a crown, and a bison on it and strode into the RCMP detachment without hesitation.

"I'm here to speak to John Cane," he said to the uniformed constable manning the front desk.

He was told to have a seat, so he folded himself into one of the cheap vinyl covered chairs to wait. Melissa was not a happy camper, but that was just too damn bad. He understood her need to do something, but he also knew that having her around for this conversation would be a liability.

He planned to use the "professional to professional" angle to get some frank information about what went down with Erin's murder. And the chances of that conversation being as open as he needed it to be if she were around would be very small.

Why he was even having this conversation when he should really be convincing Melissa to leave town with him, to go to Vancouver and possibly mentor Nadya, was something he didn't want to think about.

The sturdy cop he'd met early that morning entered the reception area and Drake stood to meet him.

"Wheeler," Cane said as he held out his hand.

His handshake was firm, and Drake sensed both suspicion and anticipation coming from him.

"Officer Cane," he said. "I was hoping we could talk."

"We'll be in the backyard," Cane told the guy on desk duty. "C'mon, I missed lunch so we can chat while I cook."

Drake followed him down the hallway and straight out the back door of the building. There was a six-by-six-foot cleared area near the corner of the building with a barbeque in it. Smoke was billowing out from the air holes, and the scent of grilled beef filled the air.

Drake grinned. "Nice setup."

"The best way to cook a good cut of beef," Cane said as he lifted the lid and poked at the half dozen steaks with the long-pronged fork. "I checked out the Hunter Protection Group. You guys have a good reputation, if a little vague in some areas."

Drake wasn't surprised. In fact, he was pleased. Cane's checking him out meant the man was thorough. "The nature of the private sector," he said. "Some things are for public knowledge, others are not."

"I'm not talking about cheating spouses or celebrity body-guarding here."

"Neither am I."

"I also read your military file, what there was of it." He lifted his gaze from the grill and stared at Drake for a moment. "*Without Warning, Sans Remorse*, huh?"

Drake smiled at the cop's use of the Canadian Forces sniper motto. When he nodded but didn't say anything, Cane continued. "Tell me you're not in Chadwick on a job."

Drake shook his head. "No, I was here on a break, looking for some peace and relaxation."

"And now you're involved in a murder. The only murder that's happened in this area in over twenty years."

"I'm involved with Melissa, not the murder."

Cane's distrust faded, and he closed the lid on the barbeque and faced Drake head on. "I can't tell you much."

"I'll take what I can get." Movement over the cop's left shoulder caught Drake's eye, and he stared at the falcon that perched on a low branch of a nearby tree. The bird was bigger than usual for a falcon, but beautiful. "Did you get anything from the scene?"

"Not much. We found no unmatched prints, but we did get some blood that wasn't Erin's. She fought, and she hurt him." Cane gave him a look. "If you see anyone around town with a broken nose or beat-up face, be sure to let me know."

Drake nodded, a small smile tugging at his lips. If he saw a guy like that, he wouldn't be calling on Cane to come get him.

"Unfortunately, because of the random nature of the crime, it's not a priority, and DNA test results will be a long time coming."

"You can send a sample to HPG. We have our own lab, licensed, and they can have it typed in less than thirty-six hours."

Sharp eyes pinned Drake to the spot. "If you're not here working, why are you so interested in this? And don't tell me it's because you love Melissa, the whole town knows you just met her."

"Melissa is related to a very good friend of mine, and that makes her my friend. Where I come from, friends help each other out." The falcon ruffled her wings and resettled, and Drake stared for a second, his imagination working overtime. There was something off about that bird. "Will you send a sample to HPG?"

"I'll see what I can do," he said.

Cane loaded the meat onto a waiting plate and they went back into the building, finishing up their conversation as they went.

# 14

Bradley had actually been pleased when his prey's trail had led him to a small town. Big cities with their anonymous crowds and self-centered people were easy to hunt in, but small towns presented more of a challenge. He'd had to work carefully so that he didn't stand out to the locals, and he was good at it, good at blending. But things had gotten too hot after he'd accidentally killed the woman, and now he was starting to feel the strain of the hunt.

That didn't mean he was going to give up, though. No way.

From a nearby tree line he had a clear field of view of the front of Chadwick's Hotel and up and down Main Street. Through his Leupold binoculars he easily saw when Wheeler left the building. He'd thought briefly about watching him, but decided the smarter move was to wait and watch the hotel. The woman had left the bookstore with Wheeler and hadn't been seen since, so she had to be inside the hotel.

What he'd really like to do is go into the hotel and question some of the staff, make sure the woman was still in there, but with two black eyes, caused by the broken nose, he'd stand out way too much. That little redhead had known what she was doing, and the more his hunt was affected by his run in with her, the less guilt he felt about killing her.

Drake Wheeler was another complication he hadn't foreseen. But that was okay, because Bradley was a good hunter, no matter the prey.

It had been easy to get Wheeler's name from the hotel, simply by calling them and asking for the "big guy's room."

"You mean Mr. Wheeler?" the helpful hotel employee had asked.

"Yeah, Ron Wheeler's room," he'd said.

"I'm sorry, sir. I think you have the wrong hotel. The man staying here is Drake Wheeler."

It had been that simple. People worry about identity theft and cybercrimes, when really a smart criminal doesn't need toys, only his brains. Not that he was a criminal.

He was a hunter, and he didn't hunt humans.

Although he couldn't deny that a frisson of excitement had hit him when he'd opened the e-mail from his assistant earlier that morning and saw Wheeler's file. The big man was a professional. And professionals lived by a code. You can't pick up a gun and not expect to get shot at in return.

*Big boy's rules* is what his own bodyguard calls the code.

That meant Wheeler would be an admirable adversary.

Bradley smiled. Maybe he should've followed Wheeler, instead of watching the hotel. Just then, his patience was rewarded when a bird of prey flew from Wheeler's hotel room window a short time later. Barely restraining his excitement, Bradley jumped from his truck and tracked the falcon with his field glasses. She was larger than any falcon he'd ever seen, but long tapered wings, short tail, and heavy bill marked her breed clearly. Peregrine. Distinctive and beautiful, the raptor had a black hood, blue-black upper-parts, and creamy white chin, throat, and under-parts, making it easy to follow in the clear blue sky.

When the bird descended, he lost sight of her and went back to his truck to wait eagerly for confirmation. Patience did not come naturally to Richard Bradley, but it was a virtue he'd developed over the years. It was something he prided himself on these days. Hunters had to be patient, not always tracking and stalking, sometimes laying in wait for prey to come to him. Because he got so little sleep when on a hunt, it was when he was waiting that he'd replenish his strength, mental and physical, with meditation.

He was so focused on the visualization of his final goal that he almost missed Wheeler striding up the sidewalk, his long legs eating up the distance between the diner and the hotel easily. Bradley watched as Wheeler glanced up at the sky before nearly ripping the door off its hinges when he entered the hotel.

Bradley trained his glasses to the sky just in time to see the pretty falcon fly right back into the hotel room with no hesitation whatsoever.

Exhilaration hit him and all fatigue fled from his system as he started planning. Melissa Montrose was indeed a true shapeshifter. The ultimate prey.

# 15

Anger burned through Drake's veins as he stalked down the silent hall to his room. It was quiet in the hotel, and what few people were around steered clear of him.

He'd sat in the diner for half an hour after leaving the RCMP offices, eavesdropping on Mary and her customers to see what they had to say about Erin's death. Apparently no one in town had seen or heard anything, and judging from the looks he got, most of them wondered what he had to do with it all. He could only guess about that though, because he'd noticed a certain falcon sitting on the roof of the building across the street, watching him. The possibilities of what, or who, that bird was distracted him so much he'd been unable to get a real read on anyone because of his own emotions.

His own emotions!

He stopped just outside his hotel room door and took a deep breath. He *had* to get a grip on himself. Wanting her, desiring her was one thing, even protecting her was within his realm of experience . . . but caring enough to get angry was dangerous.

He stopped just outside his hotel room door and took a deep breath. He could not let this woman get to him. Walls up and thoughts calm, Drake entered the hotel room . . . and stopped dead at the sight of the black-hooded falcon in the middle of the room.

Before he could blink, the bird blurred and grew into a naked Melissa Montrose crouched on the floor. She rose to her feet, her spine straight and proud, and looked him in the eye.

"It *was* you!" he said, slamming the door behind him. "What the hell did you think you were doing?"

"What?" She looked at him, her expression mulish. "You said no one would talk to you while I was around. Well, no one knew I was around."

He tried desperately not to notice the fact that she was standing there buck naked, but temper, adrenaline, and arousal made a potent cocktail and he was already harder than he'd ever been. "*I* knew you were there."

"Only because you know I'm capable of shifting. No one else knows that." She pulled the T-shirt he'd given her earlier over her head, and his gut clenched at the new half-dressed look.

Thick, caramel-colored hair, tousled and wild looking, flushed cheeks, and fire in her eyes . . . she made him forget why he was mad. She made him forget everything except the need to claim her.

She planted her hands on her barely covered hips and glared at him.

"If you think I'm going to sit back and let the big, strong, alpha male take charge, you've got another think coming. Erin was my friend, and she was killed in my home. *My home!*" She stomped right up to him and poked him in the chest with a stiff finger. "And you are not the boss of me!"

Pressure built up inside him. Did she not get what was going on? "I'm not trying to be your boss, I'm trying to keep you alive. Did you even think that whoever killed Erin is still out there?"

"Of course I know he's still out there, and I want to go fucking get him!"

Unable to express himself with words, Drake did what came naturally. He acted.

Grabbing Melissa he slammed his mouth down on hers. All the emotions roiling around inside him came to the fore and he punished her for it. His tongue plundered her sweet lips and his hands held her tight to him as he backed her up against the wall.

Melissa whimpered as her back hit the wall, and Drake struggled to control his primal need to take her. He didn't want to hurt her, he just wanted—he *needed* to make her his.

Bracing both hands on the wall by her head, he pushed back, only to have her claw at his shoulders. "Don't stop," she urged, pulling him closer.

Drake pressed his forehead against hers and stared into her eyes. "Are you sure?"

Melissa nodded and reached for his belt buckle. "Oh yes." All she could think about was having him inside her, connecting with him and feeling the way only he made her feel.

Thoughts of secrets and lies and death were washed away by the pure need to join, physically and emotionally, with the man in front of her. His hands cupped her breasts through the T-shirt and his teeth nipped at her neck as she struggled to get his zipper down over the rigid bulge in his pants.

"Finally!" she cried. She shoved his pants and shorts out of the way .

"Oh God," he groaned when she squeezed him.

He felt so good in her hand, so hot and hard and throbbing to a beat that matched her heart. She pulled him closer and hooked a leg over his bare hip.

"Take me, Drake." She said as she kissed his neck, his jaw, and finally his lips. "Take me right now."

He pushed his hips forward and she guided him into her slick sex. The swollen head of his cock breached her cunt and she almost came.

"Fuck, you feel so good." She panted the words, unable to catch her breath and not caring.

Drake slanted his mouth over hers, thrusting his tongue in deep at the same time he rammed his cock home. His hips pumped hard and fast as he fucked her against the wall.

She threw back her head, glorying in the sensations that swamped her body. Pleasure ripped through her, making her pussy clench and every nerve ending in her body sing. She tried to pull her mouth away, to suck in air, but Drake held her there with a firm hand wrapped in her hair. The air she breathed came from him, and it was the sweetest thing she'd ever known.

His other hand slid beneath her raised thigh and hitched it higher. He bent his knees and changed the angle of his thrusts. His cock hit the magic button deep inside and she came with a scream.

When the spasms stopped, Drake pulled out, turned her around, kicked her feet apart with his still-booted foot, and shoved his cock back into her. Her pussy clenched and she gasped. "Yes! More."

One hand gripped her hip and the other reached under her shirt to cup a swaying breast. He pinched her nipple, and sensation rocketed to her sex. The hand on her hips moved inward and his thumb pressed against her puckered hole.

Melissa braced her hands on the wall and pushed back against him, whimpering with pleasure at each hard stroke, urging him to go harder, push farther.

His thumb dipped down and rubbed between her swollen

pussy lips where his cock was shafting in and out of her body. "Christ, you're wet," he muttered. "So juicy and ripe."

Then his thumb was pressing against her rear entrance once again. Slow and steady he pushed, and sensation swamped Melissa.

"Oh yes." The words slipped past the knot in her throat as her muscles trembled.

She arched her back, tilting her ass up and pushing back against him. Something deep inside her needed his seed, needed him to give her part of himself, to mark her. She bit her lip and rocked faster, silently urging him to follow her as ecstasy burst from her core and spread.

"Fuck!" Two large hands grabbed her hips, holding her still as Drake pumped one, two, three more times until his cock jerked and twitched as come flooded her insides.

# 16

Short minutes later, Drake straightened up and pulled away from Melissa. She listened to his movements as he efficiently got rid of his clothes and then melted bonelessly in his arms when they wrapped around her once again. He picked her up and carried her to the bed, where he stretched out beside her.

Mel gazed into Drake's killer eyes as he cupped her cheek in a rough palm, his thumb rubbed her bottom lip, and her heart swelled so much at the ferocious longing she saw that she wondered that it didn't burst from her chest.

"I'm here for you, Melissa. I'm not leaving you and I'm *not* going to let anyone else get to you. Understand?"

"I won't sit in this room while you go get him for me," she said softly. She didn't want to fight with him, but he had to understand she wasn't going to back down, even after two soul-shattering orgasms.

"He's out there hunting you!"

"You don't know that." She frowned and sat up straight. "Or do you? How much *do* you know that you're not telling me?"

Drake flopped back on the bed, his exasperation clear. "Nothing. You heard what Cane said, and that's all I know."

"I don't know why you came looking for me, or what you want from me, or why you think Erin's killer is really after me. You can't know for sure it wasn't some random thing if all you know is what I know."

"Oh, come on, Melissa," he said. "You can't believe that."

Melissa slid from the bed and stared down at him. Just uttering "Erin" and "killer" in the same sentence was a knife to the gut, but she couldn't back down. He needed to understand. "For all I know, Mr. Sniper Man, you're part of some secret government agency who wants to lock me up and study me. So until you give me some answers, I'm not sure I can trust you the way you want me to."

Ugly emotions roiled around in Drake's gut. *His* gut. His own emotions! What the hell was it about this woman that got to him so deeply? He wanted to get off the bed, stalk into the bathroom, and slam the door. He wanted to yell at Melissa about how trustworthy he was. He worked in a world full of supernatural creatures that were all unknown to most of society. He was an ex-soldier with secrets that could take down the government. His own ability let him in on the truths, lies, and secret desires of anyone he was in contact with, for Christ's sake!

Anyone except her.

And to make things worse. She was right.

He took a deep breath and moved until he was sitting against the padded headboard and the sheets pooled at his hips. Her gaze burned into him as he closed his eyes and tried to get his fucked-up emotions under control.

"I don't mean to be secretive," he said when he finally got a grip. "I'm just not someone who's good with words."

He could see the brief struggle in Melissa before she climbed back up on the bed and sat by his hip, facing him. "I don't need you to be eloquent, Drake. I just need you to be open and honest with me."

Shit, not just honest, but *open* and honest. He cringed deep inside, but spoke clearly. "What do you want to know?"

"You said you came here because of some notes a guy you killed had that pointed to a skinwalker being in Chadwick, but you also said you weren't here to hunt or to hurt me."

She paused, looking at him expectantly, so he nodded. "Yes."

"If you didn't come to hunt or kill a skinwalker, why did you come?"

The only place to start was at the beginning, so he told her about Nadya, his friend's little sister who'd recently turned sixteen and was scared of the magic within herself.

"You know a young girl who claims to be the daughter of a pureblood shape-shifter?"

Her wording piqued his curiosity. "Why do you say 'claims' like it's not possible?"

"Because it's not," she said. "First of all, female purebloods are rare. Even when we were at our strongest, only mating within our race, the males outnumbered the females two to one. Now that our numbers are so low and there are less than half a dozen female purebloods in the world, the chances of a female being born as a half-breed are . . . well, it would be almost impossible."

She paused, putting up a hand when he opened his mouth. "Second, as the Sharza, I know who all of the shape-shifters left in the world are. Deaths might go unrecorded for a small amount if time, but a birth would not."

"What if the father, the pureblood, was killed before the birth happened?"

Melissa stared, her mouth open in a delectable little *O*.

He chuckled. Damn she was something. Smart, tough, and beautiful . . . and still mostly naked. He reached out and put a hand on her knee, letting his fingers trail lightly over her golden skin.

His touch snapped her out of her surprise and she pushed his hand away. "We're talking."

He put his hand back. "I can talk and touch at the same time. Can't you?"

She caught his subtle challenge and her chin tilted stubbornly. But she left his hand where it was.

"Tell me more about this girl."

Drake bit back his smile and told her how Nadya's mother, a gypsy, was an exotic dancer who worked in each town for a little while, falling in love with a new man in each town. One such man claimed to be a pureblood shape-shifter, and he asked her to marry him when she got pregnant. "But gypsies are a superstitious lot. They didn't trust him, and they killed the man when they found out what he was. Nadya's mother died when she was giving birth, and Nadya was raised by the gypsy clan who feared her because of who her father was."

Melissa shook her head in wonder. "I'm surprised they didn't kill her when she was born."

"They probably would have, if it weren't for Jewel." Drake smirked. "Jewel Kattalis is one protective older sister, and tougher than a lot of soldiers I know."

"This girl, Nadya, she's able to shift?"

"That's just it. The gypsy clan taught her nothing about her shape-shifter powers. They basically ignored them as long as they could. From what I understand the clan actually feared her

106

because her magic was so strong, even as a child. We've re-searched legends and myths and talked to a werewolf alpha, but no one has been able to help her shift."

"Then she's not a shape-shifter. Her father lied. Men lie to get women into bed all the time."

"Some men do." Drake's hand crept farther up Melissa's thigh. "Even though she hasn't been able to shift, she has amazing magic. She can work any spell, and she can push people with her mind. Sort of like a Jedi mind trick from *Star Wars*. Using her own suggestions to make people do what she wants."

Melissa froze.

"What?" He stared, almost seeing the wheels in Melissa's head turning as she went into an almost trancelike state. Then the color drained from her face.

He sat up, reaching for her shoulders and giving her a shake. "Melissa?"

"You said she just turned sixteen?"

"Yes."

"Where was she born, do you know? What area of the country?"

Drake thought back over the many conversations he'd listened to Devil and Jewel have about Nadya. "Northern Alberta, I think her parents met in Fort McMurry."

"Near the Oil Sands?"

"Yeah." Fear shot through Drake at the expression of shock on her face. Her pupils were big and round, her eyes filling with tears. "Melissa, what the hell is going on? You're scaring me."

As soon as the words left his mouth, he realized they were true. It had been fear feeding his temper earlier, not anger or frustration. Fear of what would've happened if he hadn't come to Chadwick, of what would've happened if Melissa hadn't been with him last night.

He gripped her shoulders and hauled her onto his lap. "Talk to me, babe."

She looked up at him, a tremulous smile on her luscious lips. "I think your friend might be my sister."

# 17

Melissa's heart ached with the possibility of it all. It was the only thing that made sense. And not only did it make sense, it solved the mystery of what had happened to her father.

"What makes you think she might be your sister?" Drake asked gently.

"The timing makes sense." She shrugged. "You said she just turned sixteen, and that matches the timing for my dad to be in that area of the country. My dad would never just *not* come home. I hoped, a part of me always hoped, but intellectually I knew he was either dead or in some secret government lab being—well, you know."

"What is this fascination you have with secret government agencies?"

Heat crept up her neck. "I read a lot of books, watch a lot of TV. Did you ever notice in those TV shows where the FBI flies around the world, no matter where they land, they're still driving the same big, black government SUV?"

He chuckled. "I don't watch much TV."

*Hmmm. Don't I look like an idiot.* "Well," she harrumphed. "If there's a fanatical religious cult trying to extinguish my race—which there is—then I don't see why the government conspiracy thing is so far off."

Drake stared at her. "The timing is right, sure, but that doesn't really mean Nadya is your sister. You know that, right?"

"It's not just the timing. The gift for compulsion you mentioned, that was my dad's talent too."

"And it's a genetic thing?"

"Not always." She wiggled in his lap, trying to ignore the growing hardness beneath her. "Every pureblood has a gift of a talent that is unique to them, or their family line. Things like telepathy, or empathy; some can converse with animals, some have kick-ass magic and can work a spell better than any witch or wizard. That sort of thing. My dad's talent was mental manipulation, or compulsion. The Jedi mind trick, as you call it."

"Is that your talent too?"

Most people, even other shifters, feared those with the talent for compulsion, but she was relieved to see only interest in Drake's eyes. "No, I inherited my mom's talent. I can shift into anything I've made a personal connection with."

"Any *thing*?"

"Animal or human."

"You can shift into another person?"

"I can shift my *appearance*. I can't shift genders; no matter what I change into, I'm female."

"Thank God."

Melissa ignored his interruption, as well as the fingers that were creeping up her thigh. "It can't just be random. I can't just say, 'I want to be a bear,' and shift into a bear. I've never touched a bear, made a connection with a bear. The same with humans—"

110

"You can shift into another human?"

"I can only shift my size and appearance to someone who I've met. I'll get their strengths and weakness; I don't get their thoughts or emotions. It's sort of hard to explain."

"No, I get it. At least as much as I need to." He smiled at her, the hand on her thigh still unmoving, but the one at her back stroking up and down slowly, leaving a trail of heat everywhere he touched. "What about your mother? You've never said what happened to her."

"She was killed when I was four."

"By the Soldiers of Chi-Rho?"

She shook her head. "Strangely enough, in a car accident. After that it was just me and my dad for a year, then we came here to live with my grandmother. My dad always traveled for work—it was better money and it went against everything in him to stay in one place too long. He didn't like leaving me here, either. He was worried it wasn't safe, but Nana insisted on it. She told him that, if he wanted me to be raised to live a happy life among ordinary humans, I needed to be raised as one—in one place. Plus, with her reputation for being an eccentric old book lady, it was understandable that I was a bit different, too."

"You're not different," Drake said as he tucked a lock of hair behind her ear. "You're special."

Melissa smiled at him, ignoring the flutter in her belly. "You're such a sweet talker."

He chuckled and gave her a smacking kiss. "We both know I'm not much of a talker of any kind. I much prefer action." He kissed her again, this time lingering until her breath was short and she was squirming in his lap.

"Stop," she said, pulling back and putting a stop to his roving hands. "We're not done talking!"

"I told you, I can do more than one thing at a time." His amazing eyes glittered with laughter. "Can't you?"

Striving for haughtiness, she arched an eyebrow and looked down at him. Well, as down as she could when perched on his lap. "Was that a challenge?"

His lips twitched. "Just a question."

*Uh-huh.* Lifting up she quickly rearranged herself so she was straddling him. "This is better." *Ohhh, so much better.* "Now, tell me, Mr. Security Specialist, what did you intend to do with me when you found me?"

"Take you away with me, of course." He shifted his hips and tugged at her shirt until they were skin against skin, his hot hardness surrounded by her damp softness. "Not to a secret government facility, but to a private one, where you could meet Nadya."

Her body betrayed her, melting inside and leaking desire from between her thighs. She could not be this close to the man and not touch, not taste. Bracing her hands on his shoulders, she leaned forward and brushed her lips over his jaw before whispering in his ear. "You want to take me away to a private place . . . and all you want me to do is meet a girl?"

"That was the plan, before I met you." His hands cupped her bare ass cheeks and pulled her close, tight to him. "Now that I know you, I have much bigger plans."

He turned his head and their lips met, parting immediately. Tongues danced and breath mingled as she cupped his face in her hands and all thoughts of conversation fled.

Drake's cock nestled between her swollen pussy lips and he began to thrust. Slow and teasing, his cock slid lengthwise, the tip nudging her clit as the shaft scraped between her sensitive folds, driving her crazy. She tried to change the angle, tried to get him to slide into her body, but his grip on her hips was firm.

She tore her mouth away from his. "Drake, please. I want you inside me."

Eyes burning bright with desire, he smiled at her. "Then take me there," he said.

Heart thumping, Melissa reached between their bodies and grasped him in her hand. He was so big and hard, all wrapped up in silk. She stroked her hand up and down, and Drake groaned, his head falling back against the wall above the headboard.

Thrilling at the control he'd given her, she stroked the head of his cock over her clit a few times, circling it, rubbing it, driving them both to a higher level before she finally lead him to her entrance. Holding him still, she lowered herself down slowly, feeling every inch as it entered her body, every throb of the pulse ripping through Drake vibrated against the sensitive walls of her cunt and echoed through Melissa.

Once he was all the way in, she sat still, exhaling slowly as they stared at one another. Her hips started to thrust and withdraw, slowly and leisurely as Drake's eyes darkened and his breath shortened.

She replaced her hands on his shoulders, and he kept his on her hips, gripping them, urging her to speed up the pace.

Melissa rested her forehead against his and began to ride him in earnest. His thighs hardened between hers as they worked together. Drake continued thrusting up as she ground down on him, her clit getting the friction it needed to keep her on the edge.

Inner muscles spasmed and sucked at Drake's cock hungrily as it swelled massively and twitched inside her. "Yes," she whispered. Her hips jerking, her pussy tightening as pleasure crashed over her. Shudders racked her body and she panted, never pulling her gaze from his as Drake grunted, thrusting up, faster and faster, unable to hold back as hot, wet come jettisoned from his body deep inside of hers.

When Drake's thighs relaxed once again, she closed her eyes and curled up against his chest, their bodies still joined. They stayed like that for a few minutes, neither wanting to break the spell. She'd never felt as safe or as treasured as she did at that moment.

# 18

After dozing for an hour, Melissa wanted to get out of the room, go for a walk or something before they tried to get into her apartment.

"Are you sure?" Drake asked, doubtful.

Mel gave him a sharp nod. "I need to get out. I need to see the people I've known forever, talk to them."

Drake knew what she wanted. It was common for those who've lost loved ones to want to be with others who knew them. She needed to remember Erin in a positive way before she went into the apartment and remembered how she was killed. "They might not say anything to you. Tragedy makes people uncomfortable."

"I know."

Having gotten a decent feel for the residents both before and after Erin's murder, Drake suggested they go to the diner.

"I'm not hungry," Melissa said. "We ate less than two hours ago."

He put his arm around her shoulders and guided her down through the lobby of the hotel. "So we'll have dessert."

"I think we already had that, too." She bumped her hip against his.

Amused, Drake gave her ass a quick squeeze. "I meant ice cream, this time."

Nobody stopped them, but several people sent sympathetic smiles Melissa's way as they went down the street. None of them looked at Drake and he was glad for it, because he could sense their curiosity, their censure, and it rankled.

The absolute worst thing about being an empath wasn't sensing people's pain, or even taking it upon himself to heal them; it was knowing that, too often, smiling faces hid ugly thoughts.

Drake pulled open the door for Melissa and they stepped into the crowded diner. The noise level dropped immediately and people stared. Some threw small smiles their way before glancing away, others didn't even bother, and the anger continued to burn inside him.

He led her to an open table near the back of the room, glaring at the trio of men sitting at the counter staring at them. He pulled out Melissa's chair, but before she could sit down, Mary came through the swinging doors from the kitchen.

She saw Melissa and walked straight over to her and pulled her into a tight hug.

"Oh, baby girl. I'm so sorry about what happened to Erin."

Drake smiled at the warmth and concern coming from the crotchety old waitress. *This* was what Melissa needed.

Melissa whispered her thanks and held onto Mary for a moment. Mary pulled back and nodded her head at Drake. "How are you doing? This guy taking good care of you?"

"I'm good," Melissa said. "Thank you for asking."

Mary looked from her to Drake, then glanced around the crowd in the now quiet diner. "What are y'all staring at?"

116

Everyone turned away and went back to whatever it was they were doing, and Mary turned back to Melissa.

She wiped her hands on her apron. "You're a good girl, Melissa. Erin was too, and sometimes bad things happen to good people. I don't want to see you hiding in that hotel room or hanging your head because some people don't know how to mind their own business. You hear me?"

"I hear you."

Drake saw Melissa's shoulders relax and wanted to hug the waitress himself.

"Good." Mary patted Melissa's shoulder and smiled at them both. "You folks hungry?"

"We already ate, but were hoping for dessert," Drake nodded.

"Ice cream, please," Melissa added.

Mary went back behind the counter, grumbling about crazy people who wanted ice cream in the middle of December. The noise level was back up, not to the level it had been, but up to the point where Mel and Drake could at least talk without every whisper being heard by every patron.

Heat burned in Drake's gut as he watched Melissa's jaw tighten and chin lift, as if in defiance. Over the past twenty-four hours the benefits of being with a person he couldn't read had become very clear to him. His own emotions had become real and he felt more . . . connected with the world.

But he hadn't been able to pick up on the fact that Melissa had blamed herself for Erin's death.

"You can't second-guess what happened, Melissa."

"If I'd have been home instead of with you, Erin would be alive right now. Everyone knows that." She shrugged, acting casual, but now that he was looking with his eyes and his heart, and not depending on his sixth sense, he could see what Mary had seen. The doubt, the guilt.

117

"And you could be dead." That didn't seem to make a difference to her so he leaned in so there was no chance of anyone else hearing him. "You do not know who, or what, is after you yet. If you'd been home you could both be dead, and then what? Things happen the way they do for a reason."

"You don't know that," she said. "You don't even know if it's me they're after, or if it *was* random. If I'd been home there might not've even been a break-in. And if there was, then fine, they would've gotten who they came for, and a hell of a fight."

"You said Erin could fight, too."

"Yeah, but she couldn't grow lethal teeth and claws."

Mary came over and set down two mugs of coffee and a huge ice-cream sundae in a bowl. When she walked away, Drake ignored the concoction and stared at Melissa. "Do you regret it, being with me?"

She played with the spoon on the table, unable to meet his eyes, and Drake's insides turned cold. She didn't say anything, but then, she didn't need to. Her silence had been answer enough.

Mel sat on the bed and watched Drake prepare to break into her home. They hadn't spoken much since the diner. She'd tried to start a conversation a time or two, but it had failed miserably when Drake hadn't responded with more than one word answers. The big, built, and quiet mystery man was back in full force.

She knew she'd hurt him, and she wasn't sure what to do about it. But so many things had happened, so much in such a short time, her head was starting to spin. Going out had been a bad idea. She should've just sat tight and waited for midnight to come, but no, she had to go out. She'd wanted to show the people of Chadwick that she was okay, and instead she'd been ashamed to discover that most of them were whispering about her sex life.

All the comfort she'd gotten from living in a small town had disappeared in seconds.

Drake opened the heavy black duffle he'd pulled from under the bed and Mel's jaw dropped.

"Private security, huh?" she said when he strapped a complicated harness over his shoulders and chest. He loaded a knife on one side and handgun on the other.

"You really think you're going to need those?"

He shrugged and slid the still-full duffle back under the bed. "Better to be prepared."

With that in mind, Mel stood and walked over to the window. They'd decided earlier that it would be best for her to shift and fly over to the apartment instead of walking down the street with Drake. It wasn't likely that anyone else would be out walking the streets after midnight on a Sunday night, but if anyone looked out their window, they'd be sure to notice Mel since she was such a hot topic for gossip.

Pushing aside the shame creeping into her psyche, she opened the window, stepped back, and began to remove her clothes. The heat of Drake's gaze roaming over her as she stripped chased her thoughts away. By the time she folded her jeans and put them on the bed her blood was running hot and her nipples were rock hard.

"You have my keys, right?"

He held them up.

"Okay, see you there." If her voice was a little breathless she hoped he'd put it down to nerves and not the arousal ripping through her system. How did he get to her so easily?

Shaking her head, she sucked in a deep breath, blew it out, and let the magic in her blood sing. The next time she blinked she was a lot closer to the carpet.

She fluttered her wings and landed on the windowsill . . . and looked at the man in the middle of the room. His eyes were bright and his lips tilted in a half smile of appreciation.

"You're beautiful, even as a bird," he said gruffly, then he spun on his heel and was out the door.

Mel took off in flight, easily soaring up and over the town. She got lost in the joy of flying for a few minutes. Nothing above her, nothing below her, and nothing but the wind ruffling her feathers. She was alone, but it was a comforting isolation. When she flew, she felt the closest to finding peace.

The air was chill and the sky was dark, but her new eyes were powerful and she could easily see what was happening on the ground below her. She saw Drake leave the hotel and move toward the end of Main Street where the bookstore was. She did another sweep down the other end of the street, still not seeing anyone else out and about, so she floated toward the apartment and perched on the roof. The snow crunched under her claws and she let out a little cry to let Drake know where she was.

His head jerked up, but she wasn't sure if he could see her from where he was. It didn't matter though, she could see him. A sense of déjà vu swept over her as she watched him walk up the dark, empty street.

It was strange to realize that it was only two nights ago that she'd watched him, not knowing anything about him. He still had that alertness he'd had the other night, his head turning as he walked, constantly aware of his surroundings. But when she made note of it this time, it gave her comfort, not fear.

He might be a hunter, but he would never hurt her. She knew that.

Drake paused at the corner, then casually turned and hurried along the side of the building right under where Melissa sat. With a flap of her powerful wings she took to the sky again.

Doing a half circle she wound her way to the back of the building, scouting as she went. A gleam in the night caught her eye and she banked right, but by the time she got around to get a better look, there was nothing.

The bird of prey's hunting instincts kicked in and she couldn't leave it alone. Knowing that Drake would enter her apartment without her, she leveled out her flight just over the treetops to the east of the town. Something was down there, in the tree line about a mile up, and it wasn't an animal. Animal skin didn't flash in the moonlight.

She circled a couple of times and saw nothing. No movement and no more flashes of light. When she got back to her building she landed at her back door and shifted. Three quick steps and she was inside. The interior was dark and she didn't hear anything.

"Drake?" she whispered.

"Here," he said from right behind her.

"Crap!" Heart in her throat, she turned and glared at him. "What are you doing behind me?"

"Making sure it was you coming in. What took you so long?"

"I saw something."

"What?"

"I don't know. It was in the trees, about a mile up the mountain. When I went to get a closer look—"

He grabbed her by the arm. "You went to get a closer look?"

"Yes." She jerked her arm away. She wasn't going to let him push her around. "I went to get a closer look, but didn't find anything."

Standing so close she could see the muscle in his jaw twitch, and she knew he was angry. But *he* knew he couldn't tell her what to do. "Did you find anything here?" she asked.

"Not yet." He moved around her and turned on a small

flashlight, shining it around the room. "The broken table is gone, and the . . . blood has been cleaned up, but nothing stands out to me yet."

She reached for the small flashlight he held out for her and turned it on. Neither of them commented on her nakedness, but the winter chill had goose bumps raising up on every inch of her skin. Nervous tension knotted in her belly and she started for the kitchen.

"My laptop's gone," she said when she came out of the kitchen. Pulse pounding in her head, she headed straight for her bedroom.

"Anything else?"

Mel didn't answer. She opened the wooden jewelry box that sat on top of her dresser and breathed a sigh of relief at the sight of a small USB stick buried among the necklaces and bracelets. She wrapped her fingers around it tightly, ignored Drake's presence, and went to the closet. After shoving all the clothes to the right, Mel moved the stack of shoe boxes to reveal the wall safe in the back corner. It looked untouched, but she opened it to be sure.

Inside was a large leather-bound book. The stressed leather and heavy velum-type paper made it clear the book was old, and probably valuable in its own right. But it was the information within that mattered the most to Melissa.

"Is that the genealogy?"

She nodded, holding it to her chest. "I know I'm the modern girl with the database and all that, but this is . . ."

Drake's hand brushed over her hair. "You don't have to explain."

She waited until his steps left the room and then she closed up the safe, moved the shoe boxes back, and stood. Whoever broke in might've gotten her laptop, but they wouldn't find anything of value on it. She was religious about wiping any trace of the database from her computer each and every time.

A quick look showed that the bedroom looked untouched, and Mel's heart clenched at the thought that Erin had stopped the intruder from getting that far.

She blew out a shaky breath and pulled her shoulders back. She needed to be strong.

After moving the clothes back the way they were, she pulled a backpack from the top of the closet.

First the book and the USB stick went into the backpack, then some clothes. Clean underwear, socks, a pair of sweatpants, and a sweater. A quick look around the bedroom told her nothing was amiss, so she went to the living room.

The crime scene.

She really wanted to leave it to Drake, but she couldn't. She couldn't demand Drake treat her as an equal and then leave the work to him because it made her palms sweat to be in the room where her friend had fought for her life.

She moved into the living room and immediately began searching. They worked the room silently, keeping their lights low to the floor so they wouldn't be seen if anyone happened to look up at the windows. But when Mel had looked at every inch of floor space and didn't find what she was looking for, she lifted the flashlight and started to check the walls.

"Keep it down," Drake warned.

"I have to look," she said. Moving swiftly but smoothly along each wall. "I have to know for sure."

"Know what?"

She lifted the flashlight to the ceiling and didn't see anything unusual. Her arm fell to her side and she stood there, strangely befuddled. "It's not here."

Drake turned his light off and moved next to her. "What's not here?"

"The Chi-Rho symbol. They always leave their mark when they kill, so we know it was them." She turned to Drake. "It couldn't have been them, Drake. But I've no idea who else it could be."

"We'll figure it out later. Right now, we've been here long enough. Let's go."

She handed him her backpack and they moved toward the door. A strange relief settled over her, and her mind kicked into overdrive.

"If it wasn't them, then maybe they weren't after me. But it couldn't have been random. It just doesn't feel random. Could they have been after Erin? But why would someone be after Erin?" She stopped on the small porch outside while Drake resealed the door with swift, sure fingers.

"Shift," he said when he was done.

But she wasn't done. "Drake, what if it was someone after Erin and they just followed her to my place when she came for a hike?"

A warm, firm hand pushed at her back gently. "Shift, Melissa. You're starting to shiver, and we can talk about this back in the room."

She spun around at the bottom of the steps. "Don't you get it? This means they weren't after me!"

For a split second she even believed what she was saying, until a muted shot sounded in the night air and Drake shoved her to the ground.

"Shift," he yelled as he struggled with a netting of some kind that tangled around his hands. "And get out of here."

# 19

Adrenaline crashed through Bradley's system as he watched Wheeler struggle with the netting. The shifter was on the ground and still in human form. He'd been waiting for her to shift back into the bird but had shot too soon. Wheeler shed the net and stepped in front of the woman, blocking his shot as she shifted.

Bradley cursed. If he'd just been a bit quicker coming down the mountain he'd have been in place long before they came out of the building. Then he wouldn't have been in such a rush. His hand shook as he leveled the rifle and looked through the scope.

The blur behind Wheeler faded and a falcon took to the night sky, screeching angrily. Wheeler dropped the netting and ran straight toward the trees. Panic hit Bradley and he fired. The shot echoed through the valley, and Wheeler stumbled at the impact. Bradley didn't stick around to see him fall; he grabbed the net gun and hustled his way back up the mountain.

When he got to his truck, his heart was pounding and sweat was streaming down his face as he cursed himself. He'd left because he hadn't wanted to get caught by the authorities. Someone was sure to have heard the shot, but now he realized he should've stuck around.

There was no guarantee the shifter would've returned to Wheeler's side, but there had been a chance.

"Ahh, it's all good, boy," he mumbled to himself as he opened the back of the SUV and crawled inside. He put the net gun away inside the weapons box and lay down with the rifle by his side. "The thrill is in the chase."

He worked at calming himself. He needed to get some sleep so he would be sharp the next morning, because the chase had just begun.

# 20

Melissa had heard the shot and saw the gun flash in the trees. She'd seen Drake stumble, then right himself. Her first instinct had been to find the person behind the gun flash and claw their eyes out, but Drake had already been moving swiftly back to the hotel and she needed to be sure he was okay.

She'd soared over the town looking for any reaction to the gunshot, and saw none. No house lights came on; no RCMP vehicle moved down the dark street. It was weird. From her vantage point in the sky the town had looked almost deserted.

She'd returned to the hotel room and shifted, quickly throwing on Drake's T-shirt that hung to mid-thigh. And now she was pacing back and forth across the room, nearly frantic, wondering if she should go back out and look for Drake or what. He should've been back already. Just as she was about to get dressed and go looking for him in human form, the door opened and he entered.

Relief, pure and true, swept through her and she rushed to his side. "Oh my God, are you okay? I thought he shot you!"

"He did." Drake dropped her backpack on the floor and moved swiftly to the bathroom. "It went right through though."

"Oh my God! We need to get you to a doctor." She followed him into the bathroom.

"No."

Heart pounding, she swallowed her panic and helped him take off his jacket, and then his T-shirt. Before she could do more than gasp at sight of the blood leaking steadily from the small hole and running down his chest Drake had a facecloth in hand and pressed to his bleeding shoulder.

He looked up from the wound in his left shoulder and started to crowd her out the door. "I can take care of it."

She stood her ground and took a deep breath. She was *not* going to let herself fall apart at the sight of a little blood. "What can I do?" she asked after taking a deep breath.

He shook his head. "Nothing. I've got it."

"Let me help, Drake." She reached for the cloth he had pressed to his shoulder, only to have him pull back sharply.

The complete lack of emotion on his face reminded her that she'd hurt him earlier, when she'd let him believe she regretted her time with him. "Drake," she said softly. "About earlier, when you asked me if I regretted being with you."

"Forget about it."

"No, I won't." She reached up and cupped his cheek. Rough bear stubble scraped against the palm of her hand as she made him look at her. "I do regret not being at home when Erin came by. I can't help but feel that if I'd been home, she'd still be alive. But I *don't* regret being with you. Not for one second did I regret being with you."

He stared at her, his expression softening just a bit. "Okay."

She smiled. He was indeed a man of few words.

"Now, let me take care of this for you."

He started to protest, but he must've seen something in her

expression now because he nodded and gestured to the bed. "In the duffle there's a first aid kit; bring it to me."

She moved quickly, doing as he asked. She unzipped the small kit and set out the small bottle of disinfectant and some gauze pads.

"I got it," he said, reaching for the gauze.

Melissa pulled back and glared at him.

With a heavy sigh, he let his arm fall back to his side.

She put the lid on the toilet seat down. "Sit," she commanded.

He finally sat back and she took the cloth off. Her insides started to tremble and she bit her lip.

There was a small but distinct hole in his upper chest—right through the firm pectoral muscle. It was clear to her that if the bullet had hit a couple more inches to the right, it would've hit his lungs.. An inch or two lower and it would've hit his heart.

Anger, swift and hot, fired her up. "How the hell did this happen?"

Drake ducked his head. "It's not a big deal."

"It *is* a big deal. I'm cleaning up blood here!" She rubbed at the raw edges of the wound a little harder than she should've.

Drake flinched. "At least it's my blood and not yours."

"What's that supposed to mean?"

"It means, next time I tell you to shift and get the hell out of there, you don't hesitate."

She rocked back on her heels and stared at him. "You're blaming me for this?"

He sighed. "No, I'm not blaming you. It was my own fault for going toward the man with the gun instead of away from him." But all he'd been able to think about was distracting the guy any way he could to keep him from taking another shot at Melissa.

The minute they'd left the apartment he'd known they were

being watched. He'd felt the guy's excitement at finding them there, alone in the dark. He'd tried to get her to shift and leave right away but she'd been too wrapped up in the who-done-it thing.

And he'd been too concerned for her to play it smart. Damned emotions. That's why he'd gone running toward the assailant in the trees instead of following his gut and getting behind cover. Or shit, even pulling the Sig from his own holster and taking a shot in the dark might've done the trick. He'd seen where the net had come from and had a better than 50 percent chance of hitting the guy. It would've at least let him know they weren't without their own firepower.

Melissa poured antiseptic over the wound on his shoulder and he clenched his teeth at the sting. He deserved to get hit. He'd been so wrapped up in Melissa, and her grief and the powerful emotions she stirred in him, that he'd been half-assing the investigative part of things.

Melissa finished cleaning the wound and reached for one of the pressure bandages from the first aid kit. She pressed the padded gauze against the cleaned wound and started to wrap the strips around him.

"There's only one of those." Drake reached for the strip she tried to put over his right shoulder to tie it off. "Clean the exit wound and put one of the regular gauze pads on it then tie the other around both."

"Shit." Mel's curse was a soft breath against his bare skin as she shifted to gain access to his back.

Drake closed his eyes and focused on the sting of the antiseptic instead of the effect her breath against his skin was having on his insides.

"Are you done yet?" he asked. "We need to talk about what's next."

She pulled the strips for the pressure bandage tight before tying them off and stepped back. "Done."

He stood, and suddenly the bathroom was too small. Her scent, the sweet musk that went straight to his balls, filled his senses. She trailed her hot little hands up his chest, flattening them over his pecs, and leaned in, her face lifted to his, her lips parting, inviting his kiss.

He wanted to—oh Christ, how he wanted to kiss her. He wanted to taste her and touch her and reassure himself that she was unhurt. But things were moving fast, and they needed to plan.

"We need to talk," he said, his hands going to her hips.

"I know," she said, pressing her full breasts against him. "But we're safe here, right? For now?"

He nodded, trying not to notice her breath feathering across his neck or her fingers creeping over to his nipples and flicking them.

"Then I suggest we talk in the morning." Her arms slid around his neck and she pulled his head down. Once their lips touched he was lost.

His hands were everywhere, tangling in her hair, sliding down the curve of her back, cupping her ass and lifting her against him. He couldn't get enough of her.

Arms full of soft eager woman he turned and sat her down on the bathroom counter. He pulled the T-shirt over her head and tossed it away. He needed to see her—to see every inch, touch every inch, and to taste every inch.

Stepping between her spread thighs, he slammed his mouth back down on hers and claimed her for his own. Her hands gripped his hips, pulling him tight to her as she wrapped her legs around him. Melissa palmed his ass, squeezing and urging him even closer as she ground against him.

Fiery need, stronger than anything he'd ever felt before, swept through Drake. And at that moment he knew that he would do anything to keep Melissa safe. Unable to put words to the emotions sweeping through him, he set about showing her how he felt.

He kissed her jaw, her ear, behind her ear and slowly moved down her body. He cupped her luscious breasts and held them pressed together so he could suckle first one nipple then the other easily.

She squirmed in his arms, panting and clawing at him. "Drake," she moaned.

He pulled back, dropping to his knees and lifting her thighs over his shoulders. The jolt of pain that flashed through him at the move was washed away by the scent of her arousal, so strong and pungent it made his dick throb. He reached down and unsnapped his jeans. He was so damned hard it was almost painful, but it was worth it to see her, so pretty, pink, and shiny, spread open and waiting for him.

"So beautiful," he whispered. He kissed the inside of her knee and her legs tightened, her right foot scraping over the bandage at his back. He flinched and she jerked her leg off him. "Oh God, I'm sorry!"

"Shhh." He pulled her leg back over his shoulder. "It's okay. All I can feel right now is how good you taste."

He nipped at her inner thigh, then laved it with his tongue, slowly moving toward her slick pussy. Sliding his hands up under her legs he tugged her forward until she was balancing on the edge of the counter.

Laying a hand on her chest, right between her breasts, he pushed back gently. "Lean back and relax, babe."

The he went to work. Using his thumbs he spread her swollen pussy lips, then blew softly across the exposed button of nerves.

132

"Don't tease me, Drake," she begged. "Please."

"You beg so pretty, baby." He leaned in and took one long lick all the way up and between her slick folds. He nudged her clit with the tip of his tongue, urging it to come out from under its protective hood. He wrapped his lips around it and suckled, flicked it with his tongue, and nipped gently with his teeth.

Melissa arched her back, her sighs and whimpers filling the room and making his head swim. He sucked harder and her body jerked. Gripping her thighs tight, he worked harder, thrilling at the feel of her little clit swelling and getting harder, emerging from its hiding place and giving him the means to make Melissa shiver and shake.

Her cream covered his tongue, filling his mouth and making him hungry for more. Ignoring everything but the sounds she was making, he focused on the hard button in his mouth. He suckled rhythmically, never stopping as he felt her begin to tremble beneath his hands.

"Drake," she moaned. "Don't stop. Just there, just like that. Don't stop!"

His heartbeat pounded in his ears, making his head swim as he sucked air heavy with her scent in through his nose. Then he slipped a finger inside her, and she went off.

Her whole body stiffened; her hand gripping his head, holding him tight as her juices streamed out of her entrance.

When her grip on him relaxed, he pulled his head back and licked his lips. He stood, looking at the amazing woman before him, all soft and pliant and gloriously feminine.

She made his heart swell in his chest and his breath catch in his throat. He was falling in love with her, and she was in danger.

He'd messed up earlier because he'd been too worried about her feelings to notice their attacker's excitement and anticipation in time. If he'd been on his game, the guy stalking her never would've gotten off a shot with the net gun, let alone the fucking bullet that had ripped through his shoulder.

It shouldn't matter to him how she was dealing with being in the apartment again. It shouldn't affect him that she'd been eager for his touch.

He could *not* let his feelings for her get in the way of keeping her safe. Ignoring the pain it caused, he tucked his dick back into his pants and buckled up. He'd just let his feelings for her get the best of him for the last time.

# 21

Drake lifted her down from the bathroom counter with gentle hands, then kissed the top of her head and walked away.

Melissa watched him, her muscles rubbery, her limbs heavy with satisfaction, and her brain still foggy with passion. They were done? Didn't he want to finish?

Confused, she picked up the discarded T-shirt and put it on. She took a minute to wash her hands and splash cold water on her face. Mind racing, she studied her reflection in the mirror. She'd missed something. What had she missed?

Taking a deep breath, she went into the bedroom to find Drake seated in the desk chair, facing the bed.

She climbed onto the bed, sat cross-legged in the middle of it, and pulled a pillow onto her lap. "What just happened?" she asked him.

He raised his eyebrows. "I made you come."

She blushed, but didn't give up. "After that."

"Nothing."

They stared at each other and she debated with herself

quickly. "I told you I didn't regret being with you. I thought you understood?"

"I do."

Then what the hell was going on?

"Ugh!" Frustration erupted and she threw the pillow at him, barely clinging to what little patience she had left. "Would you stop with the strong and silent routine and talk to me?"

He exploded from the chair and it fell back behind him, hitting the desk.

"What do you want me to say, Melissa? That I'm falling in love with you? That it's my fault you almost got caught tonight? Possibly killed? Do you want to hear that you mess with my head so much I can't think straight when you're around? Does it make you feel better to know all of that?"

Stunned, she stared at him. He was falling in love with her?

"Drake," she said softly.

"Stop." He held up a hand. "You don't need to tell me it's too fast. Too much too soon. I *know* that."

Melissa's heart pounded as he paced back and forth in front of her, words spilling from his lips nonstop.

"How can I be falling for you when I barely know you, right? But I really know all I need to know. You're smart and sassy and loving and loyal. You're strong and courageous and so fucking beautiful you take my breath away."

He stopped his pacing and looked at her on the bed, his emerald eyes shining bright with emotion. "You make me feel so much."

"Drake—"

"But your life is in a tailspin, and you can't possibly know what's real and what's just reaction to it all. And how can you ever look at me, be with me, and not remember the night your best friend was murdered?" He shook his head. "It's best to shut it down now. To get you out of here. You need to be somewhere safe. Then we'll find out who's done this, who's after you. And when we do, I'll take care of it."

He righted the desk chair and sat back down, as if everything were settled.

Melissa blew out the breath she'd been holding. "Wow!" she said. "You have it all figured out, don't you?"

She wasn't sure if she was mad, flattered, or insulted. Her hands clenched in her lap as she sucked in a deep breath, and decided to go with mad.

"The big, strong man is going to come into town and sweep me away to safety. Then you'll solve all my troubles for me while I sit where? In a safe house somewhere?" She rocked up on her knees. "No way, buster!"

"Melissa—"

"No! You've had you're turn, now it's mine. You sit there and listen, and listen *good*. I'm only telling you this one more time, and if it doesn't get through your thick skull, then I'm walking out that door right now. Got it?"

He glared at her.

"Got it?" she asked through clenched teeth.

"Got it."

"I am not going to sit back and let someone else, *anyone* else, do what is mine to do. Erin was my friend, and the only family I had left. And she was killed because of it. Whoever is after me is royally fucked, because I'm done hiding, I'm done playing it safe, and I am going after the bastard. If you aren't going to help me, then get the hell out of my way."

She stopped yelling and stared at Drake, her chest heaving with all the stirred-up emotions. After a couple seconds of silence she sat back on her knees, the fight gone out of her.

"And about us . . . I don't know exactly *what* is happening between us, but I do know that I'm smart enough to separate our getting together with Erin getting killed. Yes, they happened on the same day, but they are not connected events, and I know that." She tilted her head and looked at him, pleading with him to understand where she was coming from. "You called me smart, so give me some credit."

Neither of them spoke for a few moments, both just looking at each other, thinking their thoughts, wondering what the other was thinking.

Then Drake leaned forward. "I'd like to you to leave town with me."

"Why?"

"Here in town this guy has the advantage, and we need to take it away from him."

Breathing a sigh of relief at the even tone of the conversation, she spoke freely. "But don't we, or I, have the advantage here? I mean, it is my home turf, so to speak."

"Yes, but you said yourself that your best fighting skill, your best weapon, is that you can grow lethal fangs and claws. Unless you want to come out as a shape-shifter to the entire town, you have no advantage here."

She understood what he was saying. What if something happened in public, or in view of people she didn't want to know her secret?

"I'd like to take you to Vancouver."

She thought about it and shook her head. "No, if we go to the city we have the same problem. Being in the middle of the city full of people."

Drake gave her a steady look. "If you stay here, the chances of someone else getting hurt are pretty high."

Damn, he knew just what button to push.

"Okay. I think you're right, we need to get out of town, and we need to do it openly, so this guy follows us. We know it's not the Chi-Rho, so who is it, and how do we know there's only one of them?" She eyed him. "Do you think it's . . ."

His lips twitched. "Do I think what? That it might be some government agent sent to trap you and bring you back to their hidden lab?"

"Don't laugh! I notice the first shot was a net, not a bullet. Whoever it was shot at you, but when they wanted me they used a net—" She stopped dead.

"Ugh!" She slapped her forehead. "What an idiot! He used a net that was just the right size for a bird."

Drake nodded, not saying anything. Not even *I told you so*.

She looked down at her hands. She'd decided she wanted his help before she even knew he was ex-military, then she'd discarded every piece of advice he'd given her. Ignored his warnings and done what she'd wanted anyway. And their adversary had used it to his advantage. If that net had landed on her when she was in falcon form, she probably wouldn't have been able to shift back without hurting herself.

She let go of all of her previous anger, and her pride. "Okay. I get that I need to listen to you, but you need to share with me too."

He nodded. "Deal."

"So, what's next?"

After debating the pros and cons of leaving town for another ten minutes Melissa finally agreed when she realized Drake was talking about going to the HPG training compound and not right into city.

"You train on a farm?"

He smiled. "Yes. We do a lot of shooting and . . . well, some strange things, so we need to be unobserved."

"You said you guys hunt the things that go bump in the night."

"Yeah."

"Is your partner, Devil, ex-military as well?"

He paused. He wasn't used to being so open with someone, but she'd made it clear that she was trusting him, so he felt it was time to meet her halfway.

"Devil's like a brother to me. We met in boot camp and went through eight years in the armed forces together before we both left to work for HPG. I was adopted, and not close to the nice family who raised me. Devil and his sister, Gina, became my family." He stared into her eyes. "I get how you feel about Erin."

She nodded. "So you trust him."

"With my life."

They decided they'd have breakfast at the diner and make it clear she was going out of town for a while. "We need everyone in town to know you're leaving tomorrow afternoon."

Melissa nodded. "I'll tell Mary, and the rest of the town will know within an hour."

"The joys of living in a small town," Drake said.

She smiled and shrugged. She'd always been glad her Nana had insisted she stay. She didn't want to think of what life would've been like growing up without Erin, or the mountain as a backyard to play in.

A wave of sadness washed over her. The mountain was still there, but she was fast learning what life without Erin was like.

"Can I use your computer?" she asked after taking a minute to get her throat working again.

"Go for it." He opened his laptop before standing so she could have his chair.

Melissa climbed from the bed with a lithe grace that made him wish she was climbing over him, naked. He bit back a groan as she bent to retrieve the USB stick out of her backpack and moved to pull the straight back chair from the corner of the room and over to the desk so he could watch her work.

He was impressed when she pulled up the data and accessed her shape-shifter database. Her fingers were swift, flying over the keyboard with confidence as she sent out a call for everyone to check in. She also issued a warning that there was a new threat, an unknown as of yet, so everyone should be hyperalert.

"See this?" she asked, pulling open a file that had a simple black symbol on it. It looked like a capital P with a long tail and an x over the tail. Melissa clicked through a couple of photos of the same symbol, spray-painted on walls, on cars, on the door of a building. "Look familiar at all?"

He shook his head. "What is it?" Whatever it is, he didn't like it. He knew it was impossible, but it sure felt like there were bad vibes coming from the images.

"That's the first two letters of the word Christ, but in the Greek alphabet, and superimposed." She looked at him. "The calling card for the Soldiers of Chi-Rho. I didn't see it at the apartment, but you spent more time in the . . . in the living room, so I wanted to make sure I didn't just miss it."

He eyed her. "It's natural for you to almost wish you'd missed it, y'know."

She started. "Are you a mind reader?"

He bit back a smile. "No. But most people prefer the enemy they know to the one they don't."

She nodded, and he saw her shoulders relax a little, and that made him feel good. It had been easy to be there for her when she was in shock, or when she was obviously grieving, and he was happy he could make her feel just a little better, without the help of his empathy.

Melissa opened some more files and showed him what she'd gathered on the religious group over the years. By the time she'd showed him everything he agreed with her completely.

The good news was, it wasn't one of the Chi-Rho who was after her now. The bad news was, they didn't know who else it could be.

He glanced at the clock and saw it was almost four in the morning. "Let's get some sleep. We should hit the diner for an early breakfast in a couple of hours, give the news time to circulate."

"Sounds good."

Melissa removed the data stick and he shut down the computer. Getting ready for bed was a bit awkward. He'd never had a long-term relationship, aside from Linda, who he never actually slept with. He'd never spent the full night at a woman's place and never had one spend the full night at his.

He and Melissa had been pretty much inseparable for the better part of three days, and now that he'd acknowledged his growing feelings for her, he wasn't sure what to do.

For the first time since he could remember, he was *feeling* things, and he wasn't entirely happy about it.

Part of him wanted desperately to wrap his arms around Melissa, carry her to the bed, and make slow, sweet love to her for the next couple of hours until they couldn't see straight. But he knew doing that could get them both killed. He had to keep his emotions in check.

He waited until she climbed into bed, still wearing his T-shirt, then he went to the bathroom and took a long cold shower, trying to figure out if he was pleased or disappointed that she hadn't brought up his confession of love, or almost love.

After drying off, he put on a clean pair of boxers and walked into the bedroom. She was curled up on her side, facing the middle of the bed and looking all warm and enticing. Drake slipped between the sheets and lay on his back, his hands behind his head so he didn't reach for her.

He tried to sleep, but he was strung too tight, tension holding him rigid to keep from reaching for her—until Melissa moved over, curled against his side, and let out a heavy sigh as she drifted deeper into sleep.

Once her body was warm against his, everything in him relaxed, and he dozed off with his arms around her.

# 22

———————

Gina studied the sketch in front of her and tried to figure out what was missing. Normally she'd think it was missing color, being a charcoal work, but the stark simplicity is what made it special. Most of her artwork came from her imagination, but occasionally they came from dreams. This one was from a dream and she hadn't quite gotten it, not yet.

Then again, wilderness art wasn't exactly her specialty.

She skimmed her pencil over the background, already knowing that the bird soaring above the trees was perfect. Whatever was missing was missing in the background, or on the ground. On the ground. Yes.

In a moment of lucidity she remembered the man on the ground in her dream. Her hand moved across the page without conscious thought, following the image in her mind, and a man began to emerge. He was standing in a clearing, his head tilted back as he watched the bird soar above him. The lines of his body relaxed and a small smile curled his lips upward at the corners.

He looked at peace with the world and his place in it.

"It's beautiful." Warm hands rested on her shoulders and Caleb bent down to kiss her cheek. "Almost as beautiful as you."

Gina covered one of his hands with her own and tilted her head back. "Thank you."

"Have you been up all night?" he asked, his fingers starting to dig into her muscles lightly.

"Ohhh," she sighed with pleasure. Her man had magic in his hands. "That feels good."

"You didn't answer my question."

"Not all night," she murmured.

"It's still early and we're supposed to be on holiday. Come back to bed."

Gina set aside her sketchpad and stood. She let Caleb lead her back to bed and stood still while he slowly unbuttoned her sleep shirt. She loved looking at him. He was her dream man come to life.

She'd dreamed of him for years before ever meeting him, and it was only by a twist of fate, or destiny, that they did meet.

"I love you," she said.

He smiled. His callused hands skimmed over her skin as he pushed aside her shirt. "I love you, too," he said. "Even if you are a bit crazy."

Then he kissed her. Everything faded away when Caleb kissed her, it had been that way since the first night they met, and she knew it always would. There was magic in the world, as a psychic she knew that better than anyone, but she also knew that the strongest magic of all was in her husband's touch.

When they met, he'd worried he was boring in bed, and she'd worked hard to prove him wrong. They'd had sex in public and sex in a hot tub, they'd experimented with toys and with positions, and each time was a wonderful new experience. They could do anything and try anything together, and they did.

But nothing was ever better than just the two of them, in a bed, loving each other.

Wrapping her arms around his neck, Gina lowered herself to the bed, pulling him down on top of her. He fit perfectly in the cradle of her thighs, rocking himself against her core until they were both panting and she was reaching to guide him into her.

He slid in easily, filling her with his body and his love as they moved together in a primal dance that had her biting his shoulder to stifle her cry and him burying his head in her neck.

Caleb levered himself off her and held her tight to his side. They lay in bed, watching the sunrise through the sheer curtains of Angelo's guest bedroom. Gina's heart thumped slow and steady in her chest, until the phone rang.

It was the kitchen phone, and someone answered it on the first ring, but she knew what it signaled.

"Caleb," she said, rolling over to look into his eyes.

"I know that tone," he said. "Did you dream?"

She shook her head. Normally her visions came in her dreams, unless she went searching for them. She'd gotten a lot stronger at being able to track things, and people, while awake, through psychometry.

Caleb's jaw tightened. "I'd be mad, but I know you're just doing what we came here to do. What did you find?"

"I didn't go looking. It's not even a vision, just a sense of . . . impending events. And that phone call, whatever it was, was the starting pistol."

His arms tightened around her and he kissed her again, long and slow, until her head was light and she was ready to climb on top of him.

When he pulled back he smiled down at her. "Let's go see what your brother has gotten us into then."

Gina and Caleb shared a shower, and she walked into the kitchen forty-five minutes later with a perma-grin.

"Yum!" she said. "Homemade waffles."

"Yum is right," Jewel said from her seat at the table. "I have a serious love–hate issue with seeing your brother stressed. I had to buy my jeans a size bigger last time I went shopping."

Gina chuckled and pulled out a seat at the table. Angelo baked whenever he got stressed. Everything from cookies to brownies to raisin bread from scratch. Or waffles.

Apparently, he was stressed now.

"You needed to gain a few pounds," Angelo said. He set another batch of waffles and a fresh plate of bacon on the table and sat down.

Before Jewel could comment on that, Gina spoke up. "Was it Drake on the phone?"

"Yeah. He and Melissa, the shape-shifter, are heading our way today."

Caleb strolled into kitchen and sat next to Gina. "After we meet this shape-shifter, will I finally get to meet a vampire?"

Gina and Angelo shared an amused look. "Even if vampires are real, are you sure you really want to meet one, babe?"

"Hell, yeah," he said, popping a piece of bacon in his mouth. "Why not?"

When Gina first met Caleb, he had refused to believe she was psychic. Then he met her brother the telepath, and Drake the empath, followed quickly by Jewel the gypsy who was trying to rescue her sister, a half pureblood shape-shifter, from a demon who'd escaped from hell and possessed a man he knew. There were times Caleb joked about how his life had become a fiction novel, and all it needed to become complete was a visit with a vampire, but Gina knew it was just his coping mechanism. And because of that, she'd made her brother promise to never tell Caleb if vampires were actually real or not.

Hell, she'd made Angel promise to never tell *her*.

"Drake is on his way here?" she asked, bringing the subject back around.

"Yeah."

"And?"

Angelo looked at her, face blank, and Gina sent him a mental message. *You may as well spill it, big brother. I know something has been put in motion.*

Giving in, Angel spilled his guts. Gina reached for Caleb's hand as Angelo told them how Melissa's best friend had been murdered and that there'd been an attack on them the night before. Melissa was being hunted, and Drake wanted to keep her safe while she wanted nothing more than to go after the guy because he killed her friend.

"I can understand that," Gina murmured.

Caleb squeezed her hand and Jewel nodded. "They're heading to the HPG Farm, and hoping the guy will follow. That way they can deal with him where innocent people won't get in the way."

Tension zinged through Gina and her spine snapped straight. Her head got light and her vision started to fade. Recognizing what was happening, she closed her eyes, tuned out the voices around her, and focused on the curtain of darkness in her mind. But the harder she focused, the more difficult it was to see anything.

Finally giving up, she opened her eyes and saw the others watching her. "Nothing. Things are changing and something bad is still going to happen—" She shook her head in frustration. "I can feel it, but I can't see anything."

"What do you want to do?" Angel asked.

She turned and gazed at Caleb. His eyes were worried, but his shoulders were strong. He nodded. "What do you want to do?"

She took a deep breath. "I want to go to them. I don't think they're going to make it here, and there's a storm brewing."

# 23

"You can't wear that to breakfast," Drake said when he saw what she was wearing the next morning.

"Why not? It's mine, and it's clean."

"And it wasn't what you were wearing when we had our date, and you're not supposed to have been in your apartment since."

Shit. "Well, what was the point of me getting some clothes last night then?"

Drake's big shoulders lifted and fell in a simple gesture. "I thought we went to get your book, and your database files, and see if we could find a hint as to who kil—who's after you."

She froze, hearing the unspoken words, and cringing. He was right. Did it really matter if she wore the same damn clothes to breakfast? It's not as if the whole town didn't already know where she'd been when Erin had been killed.

She glanced over her shoulder, girding herself. "It's okay, y'know. You can say it. Erin was killed, murdered, in my apartment. Those are the facts."

His gaze burned into her back as she continued to change,

but she didn't say anything more. The feel-good moment that had been born from waking up in his arms was gone.

Neither spoke as they headed for the diner. Their heads were down against the wind, and Drake's hand at her back kept her going when she would've turned around. She knew why they were doing this, but her stomach was in knots at the thought of going back into the diner and dealing with the staring and the gossip again.

Drake pushed open the door, and once again held it for her to enter first. There was a quick lull in the noise, and then it picked right up again. A couple of people even smiled and nodded at her as they made their way to one of the few empty tables.

Mary came bustling out from behind the counter, her smile as wide as the swinging hips in her red-and-white uniform. "It's nice to see you this morning, people," she said when she stopped at their table. "What can I get for you?"

They each ordered a full breakfast. Mary scribbled their order on the old-fashioned order pad. "Eating a big breakfast is the best way to start the day off."

"It's going to be a long day," Drake said. "We'll need the fuel."

Melissa practically saw Mary's gossip radar go off above her head. "Got big plans, do ya?" she asked.

"We're going to Vancouver," Melissa said. "I can't get into my apartment, and well, I think I need a bit of a break from this place for a while."

"Vancouver!"

"Yeah. Drake's from there, and I'm going to spend some time with him and his family."

"But it's just a visit, right? You'll be back here, running the bookstore, in the New Year?"

Melissa looked at Drake. At this point, she honestly wasn't even sure if she'd be back. "Yes, it's just a visit."

"Good girl," Mary said as she went off, trailing her hand over Melissa's shoulder.

She watched Drake, strong and silent as he scanned the crowd. He nodded at John Cane, who was just paying his bill at the counter. The RCMP officer smiled at Melissa and waved on his way out the door.

A couple of others smiled, but most of the customers just avoided her gaze as she looked around the room.

Their food arrived, plates heaped with fried eggs, bacon, sausage, and hash browns. Melissa didn't even try to talk with Drake, she just put her head down and went to work.

In an effort to appear normal, and sort of flaunt themselves around town to draw attention, Drake suggested shopping for clothes as soon the stores opened.

All in all, breakfast at the diner had gone a lot better than dessert the night before. Whether it was because she wasn't hiding in Drake's room anymore, or the fact that he was right next to her, glaring and growling like a guard dog at anyone who looked even remotely askance at her she wasn't sure.

Either way, Mel refused to let them get to her. They had no idea what was going on and she didn't need their approval. She didn't need anyone's approval. She walked side by side with Drake and focused on trying to see if anyone stood out as the possible attacker.

"Do you really think it could be a resident of Chadwick?" she asked Drake as they approached the sportswear shop.

It was cold enough that her words caused little frosty white puffs in the air, and she made a mental note to buy long underwear.

"It's a possibility," Drake said. "Maybe someone saw you shift and thinks you're evil."

"But I've lived here almost my whole life!"

"Some people are superstitious—set in their beliefs—and it doesn't matter how long, or how well you know them." He grimaced. "It would explain why he killed Erin. Maybe she knew him."

Melissa really didn't want to think that way, but he was right. She pulled open the door to the sports store and started inside before she noticed that Drake hung back. "You coming?"

"I'll wait out here," he said. "Take your time."

She shrugged and went inside, feeling the warm welcome of a store she'd spent many dollars in over the years. Snowboards lined the wall to her left, ski equipment farther down, and snowshoes at the back. Skates and hockey gear took up the right side of the store, with a clear path to the cash desk in the middle. Behind the cash desk, at the back of the store, was the clothing—everything from thermal underwear to ski suits.

Melissa didn't know why Drake had chosen to stay outside—despite their talk, he was still holding back—but she was glad for a few moments alone in the store. There was a little tension between them, and she wasn't ready to deal with it just yet. When she'd woken up, Drake was already at the desk, working on his computer, and she'd wondered if he'd even slept.

It was definitely weird to think he hadn't wanted to get into the bed with her after what they'd already been through together, but she wasn't going to push. She accepted that when this was over, they'd talk about them, as a couple.

Or not.

"Hey, Mac," she called out to the curly-haired guy behind the counter. His curls were still black as ink, even though he had to be at least in his early sixties. Erin and her used to joke about asking him what kind of hair dye he used, because it always looked so shiny and soft.

"Melissa." He nodded.

A tingle of unease unfurled in her belly. "How's business?" she asked as she moved past the register to the ladies' wear area of the store.

"Same as always," he said before turning away and shuffling some papers.

Unable to understand what exactly his problem was, Melissa stopped and leaned on the counter. "And you? How are you and Marla doing? Are the kids coming home for Christmas?"

"Family's fine," he said over his shoulder.

Anger burned deep inside her as Melissa remembered what Mary had said the night before. The words had made her feel better at the time, but now she realized that it truly meant people had been talking about her, and not in a good way.

When he realized she wasn't going to go away he turned and faced her. "What can I help you with?"

"You can tell me what your problem with me is."

Mac's ruddy cheeks turned even redder and his thin lisp pursed. "No problem," he said.

"Then why the stiff formality? What happened to the shop-keeper that laughed when Erin and I decided to give snowshoeing a try?"

He didn't say anything; his gaze looking steadily over her left shoulder. Mel thought he was just avoiding eye contact until she turned her head and saw that he was staring at Drake, who was waiting just outside the door for her.

"Ahh," she said.

Part of her wanted to spin about on her heel and leave without another word. But the stubborn pride part of her was stronger. She slapped her hand on the counter and Mac jumped.

go about my shopping then, since I'm not good
for you to actually converse with anymore."

ears burned at the back of her throat as she selected a cou-
e of turtlenecks, a polar fleece vest, and a pair of heavy cargo
pants that reminded her of the ones Drake wore. She grabbed a
pair of thermal underwear and some wool socks and headed to
the till.

Mac ran her card through the machine and slid the slip
across the counter to her.

She signed it and grabbed her bag. Two steps away from the
counter she turned and found Mac staring right at her.

"You know," she said. "There's no shame in a single woman
enjoying the pleasure of a single man's company. However,
there is shame in a married man keeping a mistress on the side.
Shame on you for breaking your vows, Mac. And shame on
you for judging those who haven't done wrong."

Tired and deflated, Melissa said nothing when she joined
Drake.

"Got everything you need?" he asked.

She nodded and they went back to the hotel. Once in the
room she dropped her shopping bags and crawled back onto
the bed.

Without a word, Drake followed her, wrapping his arms
around her and cuddling her close until she dozed off.

Drake regretted his choice to stay outside the store and
watch for signs of anyone following them. Melissa had come
outside with her purchases, silent and stiff. And while she hadn't
been crying when she'd crawled onto the bed, Drake was pretty
sure it was only because she was so stubborn and she was fighting it.

It was strange not being able to know exactly what she was
feeling. Even stranger was wanting to know what she was feel-

ing! The desire to comfort Melissa came from a different place than his need to comfort others. A more organic place.

He wanted to take away Melissa's pain because it hurt her, not because it hurt him.

The buzz of his cell phone in his pocket woke Drake and he glanced quickly at the clock. Almost noon. They'd dozed for a couple of hours after shopping.

The caller ID showed it wasn't a number he recognized but Drake flipped his phone open anyway. "Wheeler here," he said.

"It's John Cane calling," said the voice on the other end. "Did I catch you before you guys left town?"

Drake sat up in bed, watching closely as Melissa slid from the other side and went into the washroom. "Yeah, we're about to check out of the hotel. Have you got news?"

"The apartment is still a crime scene, but the bookstore's been cleared. Melissa can go back in if she wants to check on things before you guys leave town."

"That's good." Drake's empathy didn't work over the phone, but he could tell the cop had more to say. "Is there anything else?"

"It looks like someone was in Melissa's apartment again last night."

"Oh yeah?"

"Does that concern you at all?"

Drake smiled. The cop knew it had been them. "Not really," he said.

"I didn't think it would," Cane said softly. "Look, Wheeler, Erin's body isn't going to be released until after the holidays, it might be best if you keep Mel away until then."

"Is there a specific reason?"

"No, no reason. Just want her to be happy. Hopefully this will all be over when she returns."

157

The shower went on in the bathroom and Drake stood, going over to turn his laptop on. "I take it you haven't found any leads?"

"No. But I wanted to tell you to be careful on the highway. They're forecasting a big snowfall."

"Will do," he said. "And Cane . . . thanks."

"Take care of her," Cane said before hanging up.

Drake studied the closed bathroom door. He *would* take care of her.

# 24

So they thought they could escape him. Bradley shook his head and readjusted the sunglasses on his nose as he watched Wheeler load up his four-wheel drive.

He'd done a quick walk-through of the town earlier that morning, wool toque pulled down over his forehead, sunglasses covering his bruised eyes. He hadn't talked to anyone, but he'd listened. God, he loved small towns. There was no such thing as a secret.

Well, almost. Melissa Montrose had a big secret. He had to give her credit for that. How she'd managed to live there, among humans, and never be found out was completely baffling . . . and impressive. Everyday people weren't always the most observant, but she'd surely slipped up over the years.

Lucky for him, the small mountain town seemed to be peopled with more of the retired or semiretired and those that enjoyed playing in the snow on boards or skis instead of men who liked to hunt.

Hunting was the true test of man. Some people believed that

it was all about the kill, but Bradley knew better. He'd learned better.

There was a time when he'd paid others to bring his prey to him. Or to his private property in Montana. Lions, bears, wolves . . . trucked in or flown in, then let loose on his thousand-acre property to be tracked and killed. Then, just when he was starting to get bored with it, one of the wolves he'd killed had turned into a man—a nude, physically fit, intelligent, and dangerous man—and a whole new hunting ground had opened up for him.

He'd always thought man would be the best prey, but even he knew killing humans just for the thrill of it was wrong. He wasn't a serial killer, he was a hunter. But werewolves and shape-shifters weren't humans. And humans who protected them weren't any better.

Gossip said they were headed for Vancouver, he thought as he watched Wheeler help the shifter into the truck. He was going to make sure they never got there.

# 25

Melissa watched the trees go by in a blur as the truck sped along the highway. The snow was falling in a steady stream, and as the sky darkened, the sight of pure white flakes coming at them in the piercing beams of the headlights was almost hypnotizing. It reminded her of warp speed from *Star Trek*.

The roads were slick though, and Drake was going nowhere near warp speed. They had a long, slow drive ahead of them, and so far, it had been a silent one.

She'd come out of the shower and Drake had told her they could go to the bookstore if she wanted before they left town, but she'd declined. There wasn't anything there that mattered to her. Not anymore. She'd thought of the bookstore as home for so long, but she'd also thought of Chadwick as home. She'd thought of people like Mac as family, or at the very least, friends.

She wasn't sure what to think anymore.

She must've zoned out watching the snow because the next thing Melissa knew, Drake was pulling off the highway onto a service road full of gas stations and fast-food restaurants that stood out like neon in the dark night.

"Hungry?" he asked.

"I could eat." She realized it was true.

Drake drove along the service road, passing McDonald's and Tim Hortons donut shop before pulling into a gas station with a diner attached. He filled up the truck and she went into the diner to get them a table.

"What can I get you, sweetie?" the waitress asked, pen in one hand, pad of paper in the other.

"Two coffees, please."

"Cream?"

Melissa realized she didn't even know how Drake liked his coffee. "Umm, sure." At least she knew he drank the stuff.

The door swung open and Mel watched as Drake strode into the place. His head swung unerringly to her and his feet followed.

She watched him walk toward her, and her heart kicked against her ribs. He was one prime male.

Big, blond, and built, she'd thought when she first saw him in her bookstore. Saliva had pooled in her mouth then, and it did so once again as she let her gaze roam up over his long legs and trim hips to his broad chest and wide shoulders.

A chest she'd cuddled against more than once in the past couple of days.

"Hey," he said when he settled into the chair across from her.

"Hey, yourself."

"What are you thinking?" he asked. "I think I like that look in your eye."

She blushed. Blushed!

"I was just enjoying the view," she said.

Drake's lips twitched and she grinned. "You're pretty hot, y'know."

His eyes widened and she giggled. "Erin called you Mr. Hot and Sexy Stranger."

"Yeah?"

"Yeah."

"And what did you call me?"

The waitress set their coffees down and looked at them expectantly. "Ready to order?"

They both ordered burgers and fries and she left the table, plastic menus tucked under her arm.

Melissa expected Drake to pick the conversation back up where they'd left off, but when he spoke he took it in a whole 'nother direction. "It's good to see you smile again."

She nodded, unsure what to say to that.

"Do you want to tell me what you've been thinking about the last few hours?"

Melissa was surprised at how easily her thoughts tumbled from her mouth.

"I don't know if I'm more hurt, or angry, or just plain disappointed," she said after she told him about Mac's treatment in the sports store that morning. "This is a man who taught us how to lace up our first pair of skates, and he didn't even mention Erin. Erin always told me the town was full of 'old fuddy duddies,' but I never saw it. I mean . . . I know they're a bit pious, and certainly nosy. But I never expected them to shun me. And it pisses me off that they won't even say something to me. Why are they shunning me? What is their problem? Is it because Erin died in my apartment? Is it because I was with you, a stranger in town, or would they have reacted if I'd been with anyone?" She sighed. "I'm just . . ."

"Every town and every city has people like that. I know it sounds trite, but think about those people that are your friends."

She tilted her head at him and raised an eyebrow. "Yeah? Did someone come knocking on your door checking on me that I wasn't aware of?"

"No, but Mary is your friend. And so is Terry; she was sincere when she said good-bye. The guy manning the desk was sad to see you go, too. Even Cane called me to make sure I took good care of you."

Melissa shrugged. She wanted to believe him. She really did. She was just so hurt. . . .

He reached across the table and lifted her chin, making her look him straight in the eye. "There are people in that town who love you, Melissa. Don't let a couple of assholes chase you from your home."

"How do you know that for sure?"

He hesitated for the briefest of moments. "I'm an empath. I can tell when someone is sincere in what they're saying."

Amazed, Melissa stared at him until he began to squirm. "An empath?"

He nodded, and for the first time, she saw uncertainty in him. "That actually explains a lot." Like his easy acceptance of the paranormal, and how he'd known exactly how to touch her body to set her on fire.

"Before you get too weirded out," he said. "I can't read you."

"Really?"

Their burgers arrived, neither speaking as the waitress set the fully loaded plates down.

"I didn't know it at first, either. In fact, the first time I saw you, I didn't know that the attraction I was feeling for you was all my own. I thought it was a combined heat from us both."

"You can't tell who the emotions you're feeling are coming from?"

164

"Usually it's easy to differentiate, but there are times when I get tired or stressed and my mental walls start to fail. I lose control of them and I can't shield myself." He picked up his burger. "That's one of the reasons why I volunteered to go to Chadwick to see if there was indeed a skinwalker or shapeshifter there."

She remembered what he'd said that first day in the bookstore. "You like isolation."

He nodded.

"And you can't read me?"

"Nope. I figure it's a pureblood thing. I can't always read Nadya, and even when I can, it's difficult."

"You said you've had a run-in with a werewolf before."

"I can read them."

"And you've had this your whole life?"

He nodded. "Why do you find it so fascinating? You said that purebloods have different abilities or talents. Surely you've met one with empathic abilities before?"

"Yeah, but I've never met a straight human with paranormal abilities before."

"Get used to it," he said around a mouthful of french fry.

She asked him what he meant.

"Devil's a telepath and Gina's a psychic—as in dreams and premonitions that come true."

Her jaw dropped and Drake chuckled. "Don't worry, none of us can shape-shift."

She threw a fry at him. "That's so not what I was thinking." What she was thinking was that, with Drake's friends, she probably wouldn't feel like such an oddity.

Drake might not be able to read her, but she'd always felt comfortable with him. *Well,* she squirmed in her seat. *As comfortable as one could be around a man who could make her panties wet with nothing more than a glance.*

# 26

Drake did his best not to get his hopes up, but by the time they'd finished their burgers, he was completely in love with Melissa Montrose.

There was no use telling himself it was too soon or that he'd be better able to protect her if he kept his emotions in check. He wasn't an idiot and he knew when he was fighting a losing battle. He might be able to build his walls and shut out other people's emotions when he needed to, but somehow, Melissa had completely blown past even his inner walls, and he couldn't hide from his own feelings any longer.

But that didn't mean he was going to tell her about them.

They stood and he watched her hips sway as she headed to the restroom before they got back on the road. The woman had one man stalking her already; she didn't need to worry about a lovesick suitor as well.

He paid the bill and waited by the door for her.

"Ready?" he asked when she joined him.

"As ever," she replied.

They zipped up their jackets and headed out. As they crossed the parking lot, Drake became aware of a tingle at the back of his neck. He lowered his shields and searched, finding his watcher.

He helped Melissa into the truck, then went around to his side. He started the engine and stepped back out to sweep the snow off the windshield with his good arm. His shoulder was sore, and any movement was uncomfortable, but he'd been injured worse and motivated less.

As he brushed away the frozen powder that had covered the windshield, a buzz of emotion caught his attention.

As he moved around the truck, he tried to pinpoint the vehicle the electric excitement was coming from, but he couldn't. It wasn't a steady vibe, just a blast here and there. Enough to tell Drake that their adversary had taken the bait and followed them out of town.

Unfortunately, he'd caught up to them sooner than Drake would've liked.

He climbed back into the truck and prepared to hit the road.

"Drake," Melissa said, reaching out and putting her hand on his before he could put the truck into gear.

He looked over at her.

"Thank you. For everything."

He didn't know what to say to that, so he didn't say anything. He smiled and put the truck in gear.

Ten kilometers down the highway, he knew they were in trouble.

"Buckle up, Melissa."

"Huh?"

He watched the bright headlights closing in on them from behind. Fast. "Our guy took the bait and he's not waiting until we stop for the night to make his move."

"Shit!"

Drake cursed himself as he split his focus between the road ahead of him and the vehicle behind them. He should've expected this. He should've known better!

"Here it comes," he warned a split second before they were hit from behind.

The wheel jerked in his hands, the ass end of the truck swung a bit, but despite the jolt to his shoulder, he maintained control of the truck. "Watch the road ahead, Melissa. Look for a pull out, or a rest station, anywhere we can head for safe ground."

He saw the headlights gaining again and cursed. Instead of slowing as he went into the next curve, his foot pressed down on the pedal and the truck jumped, swinging a bit as they rounded the bend, but not getting hit from behind.

As soon as they were out of the turn, the other truck picked up again and this time hit their rear quarter panel at an angle. "Hang on to your seat belt!" he yelled as the truck skidded and went off the highway.

They accelerated head first for a few yards, their headlights bouncing wildly from ground to air before they hit a harsh ledge and the truck flipped, rolling once before slamming into a copse of trees.

Pain exploded in Drake's head and he fought to stay conscious in the deafening silence. Turning his head he looked over to see Melissa, her eyes closed and head lolling against the passenger side window.

"Melissa," he said, struggling to speak as everything went black.

Mel thought she heard her name.

"Drake?" she called out, swimming through the fog in her head. She opened her eyes, and pain flashed through her head. She groaned, putting her head up and probing her forehead tentatively. Her fingers came away wet, but not dripping blood. "I'll live," she muttered.

She looked over and saw Drake passed out. Galvanized by the fear that pierced her heart, she struggled with her seat belt.

"Fuck!" she shouted. As if the curse were a magic word, the belt released and she turned to Drake. She touched his forehead, where a small cut was leaking a steady flow of blood. "Drake? Can you hear me?"

He moaned and she kept talking. "That's it, Drake. Come on, wake up for me. Don't leave me here alone."

That did it. His lids fluttered and she saw his gorgeous green peepers staring at her.

"You okay?" he asked.

"Yeah. A hell of a headache, but other than that I'm fine."

"How long was I out?"

"I don't know, no more than a minute or two I think."

"Okay, we need to move. We can't stay here. This guy isn't going to sit up there and wait, he's going to find a way to come down here and get us."

"My door is jammed," she said, after trying to get it open with no luck.

Drake heaved his body and his door swung open. He slid out of the truck with a grunt and after a moment, gestured for her to follow. "Quick," he commanded.

She scrambled across the seats, pulse thundering in her ears as she struggled to stay calm. They were going to be all right. They weren't hurt and they weren't alone. They had each other.

"Okay," she said when she was standing outside in the wind and snow. "Now what?"

Drake tried his cell phone but got no signal. He looked at her. "You need to shift."

"Why?"

"I want you to get out of here."

"No way, I'm not leaving you here."

"Melissa."

"What? Fly away and leave you here?"

"You need to go get help."

She brushed her hair out of her face and glared at him through the falling snow. "I'm not leaving you here with some maniac who's after me to start with."

"You have to." He pointed, and Melissa looked down.

"Holy fuck." Her head swam at what she thought she was seeing. "Is that your shin?"

Through the falling snow, she could see the awkward angle of the bottom half of his left leg. When she bent down to look closer she realized that it wasn't snow sticking to his pants, it was a chunk of bone. Broken bone had poked right through the material and was exposed to the raging elements.

She snapped her head back and took a better look at Drake. "Oh man," she said. "Damn. Okay, your first aid kit . . . where's your first aid kit?"

"Melissa, I want you to shift and get out of here. This guy isn't after me, he's after you."

"I can't leave you like this!"

"Yes, you can."

"Well, I won't." She stepped closer, getting up in his face. "Don't even try to make me go away right now, Drake Wheeler. Just shut the hell up and help me fix this."

He chuckled. "You can't fix this, Melissa. You're not a doctor."

"Okay. Fix it was the wrong term. But I can do *something* about it," she muttered as she reached past him into the truck, searching for the first aid kit he'd had at the hotel.

"You need to shift and go get help."

"Would you stop with that?" She stepped back into the wind and threw her hands in the air. "Who the fuck am I going

171

to go and get? We're out in the middle of nowhere, down the side of the mountain."

"Melissa." He gripped her arm, and she noticed the way his lips were compressed. "You said you'd listen to me. You agreed that, when I told you to shift and get the fuck out, you'd go."

"I lied!"

They glared at each other for a minute before Melissa gave in, sort of. "Okay. Let's be smart," she said.

"Yes, let's"

She glared.

"Let's get you away from the truck, to a safe spot, then I'll go for help. How's that?"

"Do I have a choice?"

She didn't even think about it. "No."

"Then let's do it."

She put up a hand, halting his jerky movements. "Before we move you, I need to fix that."

He glared. She glared. Finally he reached behind the seat of the truck awkwardly and pulled out the first aid kit. He also pulled out a long black case. He lifted it up and balanced it on the side of the truck. "Hold this steady a minute."

She moved beside him. Before she could ask what he was doing he unsnapped the case and lifted the lid.

"Is that a gun?"

"It's more than a gun, baby." He pulled the huge thing from the case and ran his hand over it lovingly. "It's Prairie Gunworks *Timberwolf*."

"It's a rifle."

"The best there is," he said. He braced the thing on the edge of the truck and starting attaching pieces from the case. She had to admit, the sight of him all macho and manly, the strong snap as he slid the pieces into place, it had a bit of an erotic feel to it.

She shifted closer to him, using him and the open case as a windbreak. "You look very sexy right now," she said.

He froze. He shut the case with a slow, precise movement and turned to her, the desire in his gaze promising long hours of pleasure. "Remind me of that when we get out of here."

"It's a promise."

"Okay," he said after another moment of wordless communication. "Let's get moving."

"Not so fast," she said. "Your leg first."

He glared, then scanned the surrounding area quickly. "Hand me the sleeping bag."

She reached into the back of the king cab and pulled out a rolled-up sleeping bag. With a quick snap he had it unfurled and laid out on the ground next to the tire. He handed her the rifle and she automatically pointed the muzzle at the ground while she watched him lowering himself to the snow-covered gravel where the truck had stopped. He propped his back against the tire and held out his hands.

"Rifle, please."

He bent his right leg and propped the gun on his knee before looking up at her. "If you're gonna do this, do it quick."

# 27

Drake steadied the Timberwolf against his right shoulder and scanned the mountainside through the night scope, making adjustments until the vision was as clear as it could get. He'd been unable to brace himself when the truck had gone over the ledge, and his left shoulder had taken a beating against the steering wheel. Not only had shoulder had taken a beating, but he'd smacked his head good, and his vision was all blurry.

*Concussion*, he thought to himself as he struggled to stay focused.

Melissa muttered as she pulled stuff out of the first aid kit and he prayed.

He couldn't remember the last time he prayed. He'd grown up not believing in God, but he'd met true evil in his line of work, and he believed in Hell. He figured he couldn't believe in Hell if he didn't believe in the counterpart.

That didn't mean he prayed, though. But for Melissa, he prayed. It was dark, he was hurt, and they were stuck. He could protect himself with a bullet, but he wasn't so sure he could protect her. He'd certainly done a piss-poor job of it so far.

A hard lump formed in his throat as he watched the woman beside him. The snow was falling more gently now, but the wind kept blowing her hair into her face and she just kept pushing it back. No hesitation.

That was her. She didn't whine or complain about the hand she was dealt, she didn't blame anyone, she just did what needed to be done.

"Hurry up." He'd had to work to push the words past his tight, dry throat, and they came out as a growl. She glared at him, but he didn't care. All he cared about was making her happy enough with his situation that she would shift and get the hell out of there.

Ignoring the demands of her patient Melissa looked at all the crap she'd pulled out of the first aid kit. How could so much stuff fit in such a small kit? The kit was smaller than the one he'd had in the hotel room, yet it seemed to have more things. It was all starting to blur in front of her.

*Focus*, she told herself. *You can do this.*

A deep breath in, and blow it out. She studied the stuff again. A pressure bandage! Closing her eyes she thought back to the mountain survival first aid class Erin's dad had made them take when they started going got for early morning hikes. Brace it. She needed to brace the break before bandaging it.

Finding some more gauze pads, she stopped and looked at Drake. He'd been silent, sitting back against the tire, watching her. "Any advice?"

"Maybe cut the pant leg open, so you don't work the fabric deeper into the wound," he said. "But other than that, you look like you know what you're doing."

"The pants," she muttered, digging through the first aid kit for a pair of scissors. "I know I saw you in here back at the hotel."

176

"Melissa."

Her head snapped up and she saw the very large, very sharp knife Drake held out to her.

She bit her lip and grabbed his pants leg, slicing it neatly to the hem and exposing his ugly wound.

For the second time in less than twenty-four hours, she was doctoring him. That scared her.

Taking another deep breath, she ignored the chill that crept into her lungs and leaned over his leg. "I wish I had rubber gloves," she muttered.

Rolling the gauze pads into tight little sausages she prepared to wiggle them into place. "Ready?" she glanced at Drake.

He nodded, his eyes on the mountainside behind her.

She went to work, doing her best to touch as little as possible as she set the gauze sausages under the break and let them slowly expand to fill the space, stabilizing the broken bone.

She peeked at Drake from under her lashes, but he wasn't watching her. His eyes were roaming, scanning their surroundings for any sign that their assailant had decide to follow them down the mountain.

"You think he'll follow?" she asked as she laid some more gauze pads over and around the exposed bone.

"Yes."

"Even in this snow?"

Drake looked at her. "He'll follow. I'm surprised he's not here already."

She swallowed. "Done," she said, after tying off the gauze she'd wrapped around his leg to hold everything in place.

"Tie it tighter," he said.

"There's no need to make it tighter. It's covered and it's protected."

Drake bent forward, reaching for the end of her knot himself.

"Stop. I'll do it."

Looking him in the eyes, she gritted her teeth and jerked the ends tighter. Drake gasped, and all the color drained from his face.

"Drake?" she cried. She lunged over his legs and shook his shoulder. Cupping his cheek, she felt the heat of a fever and panicked. "Don't you pass out on me. Don't you dare fucking pass out and leave me alone out here."

His eyelids fluttered and lifted. "I'd never leave you alone," he said, staring into her eyes.

Caught by the swirling emotions in his bright eyes, she moved closer, lifting her face and placing her lips on his.

The chill went away and she sighed into his mouth. It wasn't a big sloppy passionate kiss, but it touched her heart.

Pulling way she stood and brushed the snow from her pants. "Let's go. We need to get you somewhere safe, then I want to check on your shoulder."

They moved swiftly, the biting wind cutting through their clothes fast.

She snatched up the sleeping bag and wrapped it around his shoulders, then handed him her backpack full of clothes and what was left of the first aid kit. He slung the rifle strap over his good shoulder while she stepped back and stripped off her clothes.

The second her thermal underwear hit the snow she shifted. When fur replaced skin, she gave her head a shake and made a quick run around the truck to get her pulse racing. Hot blood soared through her system and she warmed quickly.

"A lynx." Drake's grin was slightly sloppy. "It was your tracks I saw on the mountain."

She smiled, happy to see him grinning, even though he was obviously in pain. She walked over to his left side, the scent of his blood filling her nose as she moved under his hand.

She'd meant to support him, to help him walk, but as a lynx she was only just over three feet high. With a thought she shifted again, this time becoming a white tail deer that stood almost five feet.

"Christ!" Drake cursed, jumping away and almost falling in the snow. "Warn me before you do that, would you?"

Yeah, like she could talk when in animal form.

An idea struck and Melissa shifted her hooves in the snow, shuffling away from Drake. She looked into his eyes and shifted once more, this time into a woman. Not herself, but someone dear and familiar, nonetheless.

She reached for her clothes, thankful that she'd bought baggy cargo pants instead of tight jeans. There was no way she could pull the thermal underwear up over her new body, but the pants, sweater, and jacket were okay.

"Okay," she said. Reaching out she took the backpack from a stunned Drake and slung it over her shoulder. "Drake? Come-on, the snow is not letting up, we need to get moving."

He gave his head a shake. "Sorry, it's the first time I've seen a shape-shifting parade."

"Ha, ha." She wrapped an arm around his waist. "You think you can make it to that bunch of trees?" She pointed to a copse of Douglas fir trees about thirty yards ahead of them, slightly down the hillside.

"Hey, if you can turn into Mary the matron, I can make it where we need to go."

"Don't laugh. Mary might be older, but she's been hauling cases of food and beer around for the better part of fifty years. She's tough, and we need her muscle."

"We need to go over there." He pointed to an area with no tree cover, but rocky boulders were poking up from the snow covered ground.

"There's no wind cover there," she argued.

"Clear line of sight to the truck, and up the hill. Better vantage point to shoot from."

Okay, that was a good enough reason.

Drake grunted and ground his teeth and ignored the pain swamping his body as he hobbled over uneven ground with a fifty-year-old woman acting as his crutch. Finally, they reached the outcropping he'd directed her to, and he haphazardly laid out the sleeping bag. He dropped down on it and stared up at Melissa.

"Go, now. Fly away," he commanded.

Hurt flashed across Mary's features and Drake's gut twisted. He wanted to keep Melissa with him, but it was selfish and stupid. He'd failed to get her to safety. He wasn't going to just sit by and let the maniac come and get her.

When he looked up from setting up his Timberwolf, she was still standing there.

"Melissa," he said. "Come here."

She knelt by his side and he cupped a hand behind her neck. He didn't see Mary's tired features, he only saw Melissa's eyes, full of love and concern.

*It's not love*, he told himself. "I need you to go," he said. "If you stay here and you get hurt, or worse, killed, I'll never forgive myself."

She stared at him and he let everything he felt show in his face. He smiled at her and let the love he had in his heart shine through. "Please," he said. "Go."

She leaned forward and pressed a quick kiss to his lips.

He watched her quickly remove her clothes and then crouch down again. "I'll be back," she said, then shifted into the falcon.

Drake lost sight of her quickly in the night sky.

It had to be close to ten o'clock. Devil and Gina would be wondering where they were when they didn't show up soon.

With Melissa gone, he grunted and groaned and leaned against the boulder, keeping the Timberwolf in position so he could lean over and check things out through the scope when he needed to.

Just as he was about to relax back, a rush of excitement washed over him. Knowing the enemy was near, he struggled into position and took a look. His vision was still blurry but he could see movement in the distance. Someone was on the other side of the truck, heading toward it, slow and stealthy.

"Not bad," he muttered when he realized the guy had gone down the mountain farther up the road, then headed across. "That's what took you so long."

He shifted his body, trying to get in the right position to be able to make the shot. The stalker was less than a kilometer away, and while on a good day Drake could make it work, it wasn't good. So he leaned back, and watched, and waited, waited for him to get in range.

He hoped the guy hurried though, because his vision was starting to darken.

Melissa flew swift and sure. She had a plan. She flew up to the road, thrilled when she saw no one there.

No big black SUV and no crazy maniac hiking his way down the side of the mountain in the dark, hiking through the deepening snow, looking for them.

Drake had said to go get help. How the hell was she supposed to do that? She'd never flown long distances, and Chadwick was a long ways away. She could continue toward Vancouver, but she didn't know how much farther they had to go, and once she hit the city, what could she do? Land in front of the police office and shift into a naked woman screaming for help about a truck run off the highway? *Yeah, that'll work . . .*

She did a last sweep of the first few kilometers of road and saw one oncoming car that didn't even slow when the driver saw her, in falcon form, sitting in the middle of the road.

After that near-death experience, she flew back down to Drake.

It turned out to be a very good thing because she found him almost unconscious and completely uncovered as he slumped over the boulder.

"What the hell are you doing here?" he barked at her, albeit in a whisper.

"I took a look around and didn't see anyone. One car nearly ran me over when I tried to get it slow down, so I came back to check on you."

"Damn it, Melissa. I want you to go." He pushed her hand away when she went to touch his forehead. "Now!"

"Your eyes are all glassy and you're sweating like a pig. I'm not going anywhere."

"You have to." His words came out almost a whine, and true fear struck her heart. Something was definitely wrong. Something more than the fever.

She stood up and planted her hands on her hips. "What is going on, Drake?"

He grabbed her wrist and jerked her down, hard. She landed in an ungraceful heap, and he yelped.

"Shit!"

"Shhh!"

"Drake, what the—"

He put a hand over her mouth and met her eyes, his whispered words sending a chill that had nothing to do with the cold down her spine. "He's over by the truck."

# 28

Melissa's eyes widened above his hand and she nodded.

He took his hand away and put a finger to his lips. Sound carried too easily, and the guy was close. "Get behind me," he told Melissa.

She moved, and he tried to get back into position to shoot, but a shaft of pain ripped up his leg and his vision faded.

"Drake?"

He opened his eyes and saw Melissa leaning over him, shaking his good shoulder. "Melissa."

Her head fell forward and she stifled a sob. "I thought you'd passed out.

"We have a problem," he said.

"Only one?"

He chuckled, glad to see some fight still in her. "I can't—"

The ping of bullet hitting tree and the crack of the gunshot echoed through the air at the same time. "Fuck!"

"I told you we should've gone to the trees!" Melissa said as she ducked.

"He hit a tree, and not a close one." Which told him the guy could hear them, but probably not see them clearly.

They had a chance, but only one, because once they made a shot, the other guy would be able to pinpoint them. "You ever shoot a gun, babe?"

"What?" At least she moved in close and kept her voice down.

He concentrated on talking slowly and clearly but still soft. His head was all fuzzy, and his tongue felt too thick for his mouth. "We're only going to get one shot at this guy, and I can't shoot. My vision is all blurred, and while I might get lucky, our best bet is you."

She stared at him. He could barely make out her face in the dark blurryness in front of him, but he could feel her eyes on him.

"Tell me what to do."

"Sit on my lap." She did, carefully avoiding his injuries, and he concentrated on arranging her behind the rifle. They didn't talk, she just let him position her how he wanted. When she finally had the stock snug against her shoulder, and her body braced by his, he told her look in the scope.

"Can you see him?"

She shook her head.

"Don't shake your head," he instructed. "Don't move. Just concentrate on making your breathing even, steady."

He waited a moment. "Now search with your eyes, not for a person, but for unusual movement, or unusual stillness. I know it sounds odd, but you'll know it—"

"Got him." Her words were barely a whisper.

"Keep him in sight, the center of the scope on the center of his body if you can. Then slowly squeeze the trigger. Feel the pressure of it push back against your finger? Stop there, breathe, babe," he struggled for his own breath, his heart racing. "You're doing so good."

He strained his focus, ignoring his own racing heart and feeling the minute lift and fall of her back against him. He concentrated. In, out, in. "Now."

She reacted, the bark of the rifle sounded, and he caught her as she jerked back against him.

"I got him!" she cried. "He fell. I got him!"

"Good for you, babe," he whispered, then let the blackness take him.

Melissa's euphoria lasted until she realized the weight against her back was dead weight.

"Drake?" she called.

Not getting an answer, she moved quick. After twisting until she was out from under him, she touched his forehead and drew her hand back.

She shook him, she called to him, she even slapped him, but she got nothing more than a small groan and a shake of his head. He was burning up and she didn't know what to do.

Covering him with the sleeping bag she glanced toward the truck. God, she hoped she'd killed the bastard. When Drake was covered, she stripped and shifted. She took another quick flight to the road, didn't see any cars, so she went back to Drake and crawled into the sleeping bag with him.

He was still dressed and she wondered if she should strip him—body heat and all that. Body heat. Cats were warmer than humans. With a thought she shifted to her lynx form and snuggled against Drake.

She stayed with him for a while, wondering the whole time if warming him when he had a fever was even the right thing to do. Should she be putting snow on his forehead? Trying to cool him? What if she hadn't killed her stalker? What if he found them like that?

Her insides were trembling and she wanted nothing more than to shift into a dragon or something and fly him out of there. Stupid mythical creature, always messing with a person's dreams.

When tremors started to rake his body she knew she couldn't put it off any longer; she need to find help, somehow.

She shifted back to the falcon, ignoring the hunger pains and the headache the energy drain from so much shifting caused, and flew up to the road. This time when she got to the highway, there was no truck there.

A big black SUV parked on the side of the road.

Four people were walking along the edge of the highway, with flashlights trained down the mountain. They were definitely looking for her and Drake. But there were four of them. Were they friends of the guy she'd shot?

Heart pounding, Melissa floated closer, using the snow flurries and the angle of the SUV to hide. She landed on the roof of the vehicle and cocked her head, listening as best she could. She felt eyes on her and turned her head to see a pretty brunette staring at her.

The woman didn't move, didn't say a word, but suddenly, one of the men turned and hurried toward her.

"Angel! Where are you going? I'm telling you he's down here. I know it!"

The man and the woman stood there, staring at Melissa on the roof of their SUV. Finally, the man removed his woolen hat and spoke softly. "Melissa? Is that you?"

She cocked her head the other way, her heart pounding, wings ready to go. "I'm Angelo Devlin, Drake's partner. We've been looking for you guys."

With a flutter of wings Melissa lifted off the SUV and landed on the ground in human form. "He's down the mountain, and he's hurt. Bad."

Pride and love warred with worry as Gina watched Angelo and Caleb rappel down the side of the mountain to get Drake. Her husband wasn't an ex-military man, or a hunter of any sort, but he was a good strong man who could hold his own in any situation. He hadn't wanted to get involved in any supernatural intrigue, but he'd understood why she'd had to, and he'd backed her play 150 percent.

Melissa had said Drake was hurt bad, and part of Gina knew he'd be okay now that they were there, but there was another part of her that wouldn't let her forget that things could change in the blink of an eye.

As soon as Melissa had shifted and gone back to Drake's side, a psychic flash had given Gina a glimpse of them all together, surrounding a table full of food, laughing and happy. But if there was one thing she knew for certain, it was that her visions were never a guaranteed outcome. After all, they'd found Drake on the side of a mountain, not in some hospital facility like her first vision had shown. Somewhere in the past few days someone had done something to shift the events of what was going to happen, and it could easily be done again. Free will did that.

"He's going to be okay, Gina," Jewel said. They stood side by side as they watched the men until they couldn't see them anymore.

"I know." She looked at her brother's girlfriend and smiled. Angel had already used the satellite phone to call for the air ambulance HPG had on stand-by, and it would be there within a quarter of an hour. "Sorry you had to stay up here with me. As much as Angel knows I can protect myself, I'm still his baby sister."

Jewel smiled. "Family comes first, and with Drake down, Devil's not taking any chances on either of us getting hurt."

They walked back to the SUV to wait for the helicopter.

# 29

Drake woke up warm and feeling no pain. He glanced around the room, and the first thing he saw was Melissa, sleeping in the armchair in the corner of the room.

He recognized the rustic décor of the HPG Farm, knew she was safe, and drifted back to sleep.

The next time he woke up, he heard her before he saw her.

"I am not leaving here until Drake wakes up and tells me to get lost."

"It's just a shower. He's not going to wake up just because you leave the room."

How Drake loved to prove his partner wrong. Drake was grinning before he even opened his eyes. "Melissa."

"Drake!" She threw herself on the bed, her arms wrapped around him, breasts pressed against him, as her unique womanly scent filled his head. "You're awake."

"And I see we both made it to HPG."

Her grin turned to a growl. "Yes. You scared me, y'know?"

"Sorry." He drank in the sight of her. Long hair pulled back in a ponytail, skin scrubbed clean, eyes shining.

"Your buddy here took care of the hunter."

"I thought you took care of him."

Devil stepped up to the bedside. "Turns out she did, mostly. Jewel and I went on a little hunt once you were on your way here in the helo. Her first one, and we found Richard Bradley, a mile away from your spot, stumbling around in the snow,leaving us a nice trail of blood."

"Richard Bradley?"

"Erin's killer," Melissa said softly.

Relief flowed over Drake. Melissa was safe. Not just safe at HPG, but safe if she wanted to go home.

Drake nodded. "So Melissa shot him, but he was okay to walk, and he stumbled in the other direction?"

Devil smirked. "He thought the mountains of B.C. were as easy to hunt in as his land in Montana."

He asked them what else had happened, and Devil told the story. Melissa just sat by his side, holding his hand and touching his arm.

"Gina to the rescue again," Devil said. "Earlier in the day she said she knew something was going to happen on the road, so we loaded up and headed out around noon. We'd hoped to meet up with you guys before things went south, but we were too late. But Gina knew knew exactly where you went off the road."

"By the way," he said. "Satellite phones are going to be standard issue in all HPG vehicles, personal and work, thanks to you and the jaunt through the Valley of No Signals."

Things had moved swiftly once Melissa hooked up with Drake's team. His team, his family, was nothing if not determined and efficient.

"Gina and Jewel tried to get Mel to sit in the SUV and wait, to get warm and be safe, but she'd have none of it," Devil said. "She flew down to you, got dressed, and prepped you for our arrival. By the time Caleb and I got to you, she'd bound you up tight in the sleeping bag and was ready to go."

They'd used a satellite phone before even heading down to Drake and the HPG helicopter was waiting at the road by the time Devil and Caleb hauled Drake to the top. "Melissa came back with you, Gina, and Caleb, and Jewel and I finished the job with Bradley."

"So what was his story anyway?" He slid a teasing glance at Melissa. "Was he a secret government agent?"

Devil's lips twisted, and he gave Drake a look as if he'd bumped his head. And not recovered. "No. He was a rich rancher dude from the States. Fancied himself a big game hunter because he hired people to bring the game to his land, where he let them go, then hunted them down. Only the last wolf he hunted turned into a man after he shot it. Which sent him on another hunt."

"So it was just a freak twist of luck that we found the papers pointing us to Chadwick at the same time this psycho decided to use it as a hunting ground?"

Devil shrugged. "Old Man Hunter got us permission to go over the findings at Bradley's ranch. I'm betting we find a connection from him to the werewolf you took out a couple weeks ago. The one with the papers on Chadwick and Sharza."

Devil went on about how they'd found Bradley and Jewel had gotten him to talk with one of her gypsy potions. But Drake tuned him out. He only had eyes for the woman beside his bed, and she was looking a bit uncomfortable now that all the loose ends had been tied up.

Drake finally tired of hearing about how wonderful Jewel was and sent Devil a mental message. *"Get lost, Devil."*

Devil chuckled and left the room without another word.

191

\* \* \*

Melissa shifted her weight from one foot to the other. "So, now what?"

Drake took a deep breath. "Now, you're free to do whatever you want—go back to Chadwick and reopen your store. I'm sure the RCMP will release Erin's body and the apartment in the next day or two if they haven't already."

"I meant about us."

Christ, he felt like a schoolboy with a crush. "What would you like to happen next?"

Before she could answer, Gina came tearing into the room. "Drake! Don't you ever scare me like that again!"

The little fireball jumped on the bed and stretched across his chest, talking a mile a minute. Drake looked at Melissa over Gina's head and smiled. "We're not done yet," he said.

Melissa's heart pounded at the promise in Drake's eyes. She was glad for Gina's interruption, otherwise she might've started a bit of a fight with the idiot man lying injured in the bed.

She turned away from where the two friends were talking, and went to stare out the window at the HPG "farm".

It was unlike any farm she'd ever been on. Not only was it huge and sprawling in a way that reminded Mel of a college campus, but also they had their own medical wing!

Drake had gone into surgery as soon as they'd landed and had remained unconscious for almost forty-eight hours. And the first thing the asshole says when he wakes up and they're alone is she could go back to Chadwick and open her store?

That was the suggestion for what was next for them from the man who'd said he was falling in love with her only days earlier? Unless it had all been some sort of white knight syndrome, and now that the bad guy was caught and she wasn't in danger anymore, then Drake wasn't interested. But there'd been undeniable heat between them even before the danger.

192

Okay, there'd always been some sort of danger element, Mel had known from the second she'd set eyes on Drake that he was dangerous to her. And sure enough, now that he held her heart in his hands, he was done with her.

"I know you two would like to be alone," Gina said, drawing Mel's attention back to the center of the room. "But there's someone who's been waiting for you to wake up, Drake, and who really wants to meet Melissa."

Drake glanced from Mel to Gina, and nodded. "Go get her."

Gina slid from the edge of the bed and went to the door. She opened it and a willowy teenage strode into the room and went straight to Drake's bedside.

"Turned into a major klutz, didn't you?" she said as she looked down at him.

Mel's chest got tight and her breath caught in her throat. She knew instantly it was Nadya, she could sense the shape-shifter blood in her.

"Ahh, it's not that major, squirt," Drake said with a crooked smile. When his hand wrapped around hers Mel realized she'd stepped closer to the bed without even knowing it. "This is Melissa, the woman I told you about. Mel, this is Nadya."

Silence fell as they stared at each other for a minute. Mel had to struggle to breathe as she watched Nadya look her up and down with guarded eyes. "So you're the big deal shape-shifter, eh? Come to teach me a thing or two?"

"Nadya," Jewel said sharply from by the door.

Until that moment Mel hadn't even known Jewel was in the room. It didn't matter though; she ignored everyone else and focused on the teenager in front of her.

Instinct told Mel now was not the time to mention that chances were good they were half-sisters.

"I'm a pureblood shape-shifter, yes. I'm also a descendent of the royal family that once ruled our kind. Would you like to learn your father's history?"

"I don't really care about the history, I prefer to live in the present." She cocked her head to the side. "I'd like to learn what sort of powers I have. You can teach me about those, right?"

Mel felt the magic push in her brain and bit back a smile. "Then you'll learn your history, too."

Nadya's eye's narrowed. "You're here to teach me about my powers."

There was another mental push and Mel let a cocky smile of her own curl her lips. "Your mental push won't work on me, Nadya. If you want to learn about your powers, you need to learn about your history. They go hand in hand."

"Does that mean you're going to stick around a while and teach me?" There was a hopeful gleam in Nadya's eyes, even though her brows had pulled into a small scowl.

Mel cast a sidelong glance at Drake, remembering what he'd told her about the way she was raised. He's hinted at Mel going back to Chadwick right away, but there was no way she was going to leave without reassuring the tough teen in front of her that she wasn't alone.

"I'll stick around for a while."

Confusion reigned within Melissa for two days.

She spent her days with Nadya. They went over the history and culture of pureblood shape-shifters in the morning, then after lunch they played with magic. The teenager was powerful, way more than Mel had expected.

"You're sure your mom wasn't magical in some way?" she's asked Nadya that afternoon.

"I didn't know my mom at all. Jewel says even though Mom never admitted to any magic, she thinks she had some, though."

"It would explain why you're already so strong."

Nadya pouted. "If I'm so strong, why can't I shift?"

Mel explained again that in order to shift, she had to make a connection with whatever she wanted to shift into. The teenager had high emotional walls and struggled with how to make a connection to an animal.

Part of Mel wanted to suggest she try to shift into Jewel, someone Nadya had a clear connection with. After all, it was physically easier to shift to another human instead of an animal, but it was psychologically harder. It could mess with her mind if she wasn't prepared for it.

And it might not be too smart to encourage a precocious underage teenager to shift into a fully adult form. The time would come, and even if Nadya was in a rush, Melissa wasn't.

*Well, not in a rush with Nadya's training anyway,* she thought as she strode down the corridor of the medical wing. Drake was another story.

Due to the surgery on his leg, Drake was confined to his bed, for five days. She'd spent the evenings with him, but everytime she tried to bring the conversation around to what was next for them, he distracted her with drugging kisses until she had to leave or climb on top of him and risk re-injuring his leg.

But she was done tiptoeing around the subject of their relationship. She wanted answers.

"We need to talk," she said the second the door to his room closed behind her.


Drake gut clenched. Those words never meant good news.

"Are you okay?" he asked, taking Melissa's hand when she stopped next to his bed.

Christ, he hated being stuck in that fucking bed!

195

"I'm fine," Melissa said. "I'm just wondering how long I should stick around here."

The tone of her voice made it feel like a question, but Drake wasn't sure if she meant it that way.

He dropped his shields and reached out, frustrated that he still couldn't get a read from her. Things would be so much simpler if he could knew what she was feeling. Did she want to stay with him? Did she want to go back to Chadwick and the life she'd had before he ever set foot in her town? He hated the insecurity running through him, and for the first time in his life he resented not being able to sense someone else's emotions.

One surefire way to know what she was feeling, was to make her feel it. He ran his hand up her arm and tugged her closer to the bed so he could run his hand over the curve of her firm ass. "You can stick around as long as you want," he said with a smile.

"Drake." She slapped at his hand, but a familiar gleam sparked in her eyes. "Do you want me to stick around?"

He cupped the back of her neck and pulled her to him. His lips met hers and he put every ounce of desire into the kiss. He wanted her to stay. He wanted her to stay forever.

She moaned, and pushed against his chest, but he held her tight. He didn't ever want to let her go, and he had to show her that!

Stroking her tongue with his, he savored the taste of her. One hand cupped her ass while his other hand smoothed over her waist and ribs to cup a heavy breast through her sweater. "God, you feel so good."

"So do you," she said as his lips trailed over her jaw and down to her neck.

He nipped at her neck, sucked on her earlobe and rubbed the rigid nipple poking against his hand.

"Drake," she whispered. "We need to talk."

"We can talk later," he said. Right now I want to touch you. I need to touch you, baby, to please you."

She shuddered against him and he spun her in his arms. Twisting slightly he held her back to him as one hand slid under her sweater and the other unsnapped her jeans. He tucked his chin against her shoulder and spoke into her ear as his hand slid into her pants.

Two fingers slid through her creamy folds and right into her tight pussy. She gasped and he groaned.

"You feel so good, baby. So right. We're a perfect fit, you and I. You're always ready for me, aren't you? Christ, I wish I could bury my cock in your warmth."

His cock throbbed with his desire, but he ignored it. The need to please her, to show her how much she meant to him was foremost in his brain, and all that mattered was her pleasure.

He thrust his fingers deep, curling them when she shuddered and gasped. The heal of his hand rubbed against the hard button of her clit and her hips started to rock with his movements. Her panting breaths echoed through the room and his heart soared at the way she trembled in his arms.

"That's it, baby. Come for me."

"Drake!" Her hand grabbed his wrist, pressing him against her harder as her pussy spasmed and clenched around his fingers.

Her head fell forward and the grip of her hand slackened. Drake gave her a minute, kissing the side of her neck softly as he cradled her against him. When his own heartbeat steadied he pulled his hand from her pants and turned her to face him.

Lifting his hand he cupped her cheek and stared into eyes full of swirling emotions that made his chest tight.

"Melissa," he said. "I-"

"Oops!" Drake looked up and saw his nurse standing in the

open doorway. "Sorry to interupt, Mr. Wheeler, but I need to take your vitals before the doctor comes to see if your leg is ready to be casted."

Drake held Melissa close and glared at the nurse. "Can you give us a minute, please."

He could sense the woman's amusement as she nodded and backed out the door and he growled.

Melissa pulled away from him as soon as the door shut and buttoned up her pants. "I've got to get going," she said.

"No, Melissa, you wanted to talk. Stay, the nurse will just take a minute."

"No, then the doctor will be here." She shook her head, avoiding his eyes. "It's okay though. I think I know what I need to do."

She moved quickly to the door opening it at the same time as the nurse re-entering the room. Panic hit Drake hard. He didn't know why, but he knew that if he let Melissa go right then, she would walk right out of his life.

"Melissa, wait!" he called out, but she was already gone.

"Fuck!" He tried to pull his leg from the traction unit and the nurse ran forward.

"Don't worry, Mr. Wheeler," the nurse said. "That girl is in love with you, she isn't going far."

The sinking feeling in his gut told Drake different. And he'd learned to always trust his gut.

# 30

Melissa was gone and they'd never managed to have their talk about what was next for them. Between Devil, Gina, and Nadya, the two of them were rarely alone, and when they did get the chance, talking was the last thing on their minds. It was his own fault, and he knew it.

He tried not to think about her after she left. He tried not to notice the emptiness inside him. Somehow, even when surrounded by people who loved him, he felt even more alone than ever. Because the one he loved wasn't there.

"When are you going to man-up and go get her?"

Drake smirked at his friend. "Man-up?"

Devil shrugged and took a drink from his beer.

Drake laughed. "Nadya's speech patterns are rubbing off on you."

"She also thinks you're being a loser by letting Melissa get away."

They were sitting in the living room of Devil's house, watching WWE and drinking beer. Everyone else had gone out to do their last-minute Christmas shopping.

Drake turned back to the TV. "I'm not letting her get away. She left. She came here to be safe, and to meet Nadya. She did that. What more is there to say?"

"Did you ask her to stay?"

"Not straight out, but she knows how I feel."

"How?"

Drake grimaced inwardly. "I told her before we ever left Chadwick."

Devil's face was serious. "You're different now than you were before you went to Chadwick, buddy. Don't bother to deny it either."

Drake struggled. He hated all the feelings and emotions swimming around inside his head, and his heart. He wanted to talk about it. *He wanted to talk,* but he couldn't find the words.

So instead, he looked at Devil and let his shields down.

Devil was quick to slip in his head and take a peek around, and friend that he was, he didn't make a joke out of things.

"You have to go to her, buddy," he said, standing up to go get another beer. "If you don't you might never see her again."

# 31

Melissa wandered around her apartment, restless, unable to sleep. Everything was cleaned up and in its place. It was her that was out of place.

It was Christmas Eve, and most of Chadwick was closed up tight. She'd opened the bookstore because she had nothing better to do.

"It's all Drake's fault," she muttered. The man would not get out of her head. She'd hung around his bedside for days, hoping for some bit of personal emotion from the man, and he'd given her nothing.

Okay, not nothing. He'd given her sweet kisses, and sensual kisses, and downright raunchy kisses.

He'd give her an orgasm that made her knees buckle while she'd stood next to his bed. Who'd have known a man with his leg in traction could be such a devastating lover?

But she wanted more than that.

Sure when he'd first got to town, she'd wanted nothing more than a night or two with the hot and sexy stranger, but so much had happened since then. She'd grown up. She'd lost a dear friend. She'd learned she had other *true* friends, unlikely friends. She'd shot a man, and been glad for it. She'd found a half sister.

She'd fallen for the ultimate loner, and now she was alone.

Flashing red and blue lights in his rearview mirror had Drake pulling the SUV onto the shoulder of the highway.

Drake tamped down his impatience and reached for his wallet, only to stop when he saw the RCMP office that was approaching his vehicle.

"Was I speeding?" he asked when John Cane stood at his window.

"Yes, but that's not why I stopped you."

Curiosity bit into Drake's impatience. "Really? Why did you stop me?"

"To see what your intentions are."

Stunned, Drake stared. "Excuse me?"

"I want to know what your intentions are in going to Chadwick today."

Drake stared at the cop. He lowered his shield a little and discovered the guy was for real. He was worried about Melissa, and he wasn't sure if Drake's showing up was a good thing or not.

"My intentions are simple. I'm here to make Melissa mine."

"And if she doesn't want to be yours?"

If she didn't want to be his, he'd dry up emotionally and probably die an old bitter man.

"If she doesn't want to be mine, then I'll leave her alone." He met Cane's sharp gaze. "She saved my life, y'know? I would never do anything to hurt her."

And that included letting her walk away from him.

In that moment, all of Drake's doubts left him. He might not be able to feel her emotions, but he could trust his own.

Cane nodded. "I'll be watching, Wheeler." He turned and walked back to his car, and Drake put the truck in gear. He was almost home.

Drake stood and stared. She was every one of his fantasies come true. Adolescent and adult.

He watched from the street, through the bookstore window, as she strolled around the store. Her hand trailed over the shelves as she went, her head titled and the expression on her beautiful face telling him she was far, far away.

Unable to hold back any longer, he pushed open the bookstore door and limped into the shop. Her head turned at the sound of the bell and their eyes met.

They just stared for minute. Drake's throat tightened and his gut clenched. All the blood in his body seemed to be in his heart, because his chest ached at the sight of her.

Finally, she moved toward him. "Well, hel-lo stranger," she purred. "Did you come to get a Christmas present?"

"I came to get you."

His words stopped her heart. Then it kicked against her ribs and proceeded to gallop in a way that she'd never experienced. She gave her head a shake, but he was still there. She pinched herself in the arm, and it hurt.

Drake was there, in her store, claiming to be there for her.

Oh. "Is Nadya alright?"

He frowned. "I'm not here because of Nadya, or anyone else. I'm here for you, and me."

"Oh, Drake," she said.

"What do you mean, 'Oh, Drake'? I know you want me, I know you care about me. Why are you pretending otherwise?"

"I'm not pretending, Drake. I do care about you, and we both know I'll always want you. But we can't be together."

"Why not?"

She watched him limp forward, and her insides melted. He was so big, and strong; even injured and wearing a bright blue cast on his leg, he inspired faith. She wanted to throw herself in his arms and let him take care of her.

But that would be bad for her. She needed a man who would not only take care of her but wouldn't fight her need to take care of him. And she told him so.

"What's that supposed to mean? I let you save my life!"

"You let me?"

He waved a big hand through the air. "You know what I mean."

"That's just it, Drake. I don't know what you mean. I can't read your mind, or your emotions. I only know what you tell me." She smiled at him. "And we both know you don't like to talk."

"I talk to you."

Actually, he did. And as much as what she was saying was true, she knew deep down she was just going through the motions. She was Drake's for however long he wanted her. And she knew he'd want her a lot longer if she made him work for her.

"Do you listen? Will you listen? Or will it always be like on the mountainside, where it will take a deathly high fever and grievous bodily injury for you to listen to me?"

The poor man looked truly befuddled, and lost. It was the lost that got to her. She didn't want him to ever feel lost or alone again.

"I'll make you a deal," she said.

"A deal?"

She grinned and she knew the instant he understood that she was his . . . almost.

His beautiful bright eyes lit up and he held out his hands, palms up. "Whatever you want."

"I want you to prove how well you listen."

"I'm listening right now," he promised.

She flipped the sign on the door and locked up the store. With Drake following closely, she led the way through the store, and up the inside stairs at the back to her apartment.

Arousal crouched low in her belly, held back only by the anticipation. After all the times he drove her crazy with desire, the times he had her begging for release . . . she couldn't wait to hear him cry out for her.

She led him straight to her bedroom.

"Get rid of the jacket," she ordered, eating him up with her eyes as he did what she asked.

"Now the rest of your clothes, please."

Melissa's pulse pounded and saliva pooled in her mouth when the T-shirt was gone and he reached for the silver buckle at his waist. His eagerness was clear in the quick work he made of his belt and zipper, shoving his slacks and shorts over his hips and down his legs in one smooth move that stole her breath.

He was beautiful.

She knew men weren't supposed to be beautiful, but he was. He stood before her completely naked, hard and proud. His emerald eyes glowed, and a lovely flush covered his chest and neck. When Melissa's gaze landed on his mouth, he growled but didn't move toward her.

Unable to resist the pull between them, she stepped forward, cupped his face in her hands, and brought him down to her for a kiss.

She nibbled at his lips before swiping her tongue across them and dipping into his mouth to taste him. He groaned, his breath mingling with hers as their tongues met and danced, tangling and moving together in a natural rhythm that soon had them both panting. She pulled away and became aware of his hands gripping her hips tightly.

"Hands off until I tell you, Drake."

His hands instantly dropped to his sides and he straightened.

She was impressed. Drake was not a man to sit back and let a woman take charge unless he was unconscious. Mel knew that firsthand. But he'd taken her concerns to heart, and he was letting her be the boss.

If Melissa had any doubts about the love he claimed, they were dispelled then. She stayed where she was, close enough to breathe in his scent and see his nipples harden when she blew a soft stream of air at them. "Yummy," she sighed.

She reached between the two of them and wrapped her hand around his cock. Not too tight, but tight enough that she would feel every telltale throb and twitch. "The ground rules are simple, and always in effect, Drake. We're equals in life, equals in bed. Understand?"

"Yes," he replied, his voice thick with lust.

"Good. And just so you know . . . I love to hear you talk. Remember, words are *not* always overrated in my world."

A small frown wrinkled his forehead, but he didn't say anything.

She stood on her tiptoes and leaned forward, deliberately breathing hotly as she whispered in his ear. "Do you enjoy oral sex, Drake?"

His cock throbbed in her hand as he nodded. "I never got the chance to taste this delicious cock of yours. Don't you think it's time?"

That made his cock jump. It swelled and throbbed against the palm of her hand and she was tempted to get on her knees and take it in her mouth. But he hadn't answered her, so she released him and stepped back.

"Undress me," she instructed.

She stood still as he lifted her T-shirt over her head, and his big strong hands trembled as they unsnapped her bra. Her nipples ached, begging for attention, but she held back. She wanted all of her clothes off before she let him touch her.

He bent at the knees, awkward because of the cast still on his left leg, and tugged the snug denim over her rounded hips and down her legs. A warm hand cupped one calf as he lifted the first leg to remove the pants, then the other. He looked up at her from his half-crouched position, his hand lingering on her calf as she said a brief prayer of thanks for the urge to shave that morning.

She reached out and stroked her fingers through the shiny locks of his hair. He pressed into her touch just like a cat being scratched behind the ears. "My panties too, please."

Drake's hands slid up the outside of her legs to her hips. He fingered the thin elastic that held the front and back triangles of cloth together. In a surprise move he pulled hard and the elastic snapped. Her excited gasp echoed through the room as the panties fell to the floor.

Her alpha man, even when he was letting her take charge, had to show his strength.

His hands cupped her naked rear and he dropped to his knees in front of her. Leaning forward, he rubbed his cheek against her bare skin and made a show of inhaling deeply before looking up at her. "I can smell how turned on you are. Do you know what your scent does to me?"

Melissa's knees almost buckled. The sight of him on his knees for her, the words he spoke, the fervent hunger clearly stamped on his face and in the tension of his body, it was like a dream.

"On the bed," she said. She wished she could pick him up and carry him, the way he'd done to her several times. But sometimes strength didn't have to be physical.

Drake moved onto the bed and stretched out in the middle.

Melissa stood there and stared at him. Emotions that had nothing to do with sex swirled about her head and made it difficult to breathe. She knew she was well on her way to loving him. He'd accepted her, as she was, for who she was. He was even willing to do the long-distance thing for as long as she needed.

She wasn't ready to leave Chadwick, yet. It held too many memories. But she was going to build new memories, with a new family.

Scrambling onto the bed she threw a leg over Drake and straddled his waist. Leaning forward, she braced her hands on the mattress next to him and licked first one flat male nipple, then the other.

"You're still not talking. I thought you wanted to get on my good side."

"Christ, that feels good," he said, his voice hoarse. "Only you can make me feel, Melissa."

She moved her head so that the curtain of her hair brushed against his skin as she went back and forth, manipulating each nipple with her tongue, her teeth, and her lips until they were rock hard and standing stiff like little miniature dicks.

Shifting her weight farther back on her heels, she scraped her chest against his belly as she moved lower, nipping at his ribs, tonguing his navel. She stopped when she was between his spread thighs, her generous breasts surrounding his rigid cock and sandwiching it to his body. He gasped and his hips pressed up.

Melissa lifted her head and gazed at his face. His eyes were watching her every move, but his lips were pursed tight.

"Talk to me, Drake. I need to hear what you like."

"Nothing feels bad when it's you that's touching me."

"You like this?" she asked, and rocked her body forward, his cock stroking firmly between her breasts.

"Yes," he hissed.

"What about this?" She dipped her head, and her tongue flicked the head of his cock when it peaked out from between her breasts as she continued to rock.

His moan echoed through the room, thrilling her. Her tongue darted out every time, swiping at the sensitive tip. Through with teasing him, she pulled back and circled the base of his cock with her finger and thumb. She held the rigid length of him away from his body and swirled her tongue all over him. She licked up the underside, following the throbbing vein there. She wrapped her lips around the head and sucked him like a lollipop. His hips thrust upwards and his sighs turned to whimpers. She waited . . . she knew it was coming.

"Please," he gasped.

"Please what, Drake?" She squeezed her thighs together. She wanted so badly to climb up his body and impale herself on his cock. She wanted to feel him touch her deep inside, feel his warmth spread through her once again. She wanted to feel . . . connected.

"Suck me."

She opened her mouth and took as much of him in as she could. She sucked gently and stroked up to the tip, then swallowed him again. Her other hand cupped his balls, measuring their weight, their feel.

Suddenly the bed shook and Drake's voice reached her loud and clear. "No, Melissa. Please!!"

She kept going, sliding her mouth up and down his cock, tasting his flavor and feeling him swell even larger in her mouth. "Melissa, damn it. Ride me, fuck me . . . love me!"

209

An arrow of pure joy went straight to her heart. It wasn't that he was begging, it was what he was begging for, it was what she wanted too. Before she could think twice, she climbed on top of him, aimed his cock at her entrance, and sank down onto him. She had to bite her tongue to keep from shouting *yes* as their connection solidified and her world righted itself.

They were together, just as they were meant to be.

# EPILOGUE

Drake Wheeler leaned back in his chair and surveyed the crowd of people around the dinner table, contentment heavy in his soul. It was Christmas 2009, and the room was full of cheer.

Only a year ago, being around this many people, even ones he loved, would have driven him slightly crazy. But not anymore.

"Are you full, Drake? Angel made dessert so I hope you saved some room." Gina said as she rested her hand on her hugely rounded belly.

Devlin strode into the room, cocky grin in place and shooting off the contentment vibe like a firecracker.

"Cheesecake or apple pie," Jewel said from across the table. "I don't know how I'm going to choose between the two."

Nadya looked up from her plate of turkey dinner. "I plan on having a piece of each."

Melissa grinned at her. "As you should. Shifting burns a lot of calories, and now that you've made your connection with your spirit animal, I know you'll be shifting all the time."

Warmth seeped into Drake's veins and flowed through his

system as he listened to the group continue. Caleb got up from the table and went for another bottle of wine, kissing his wife's cheek and murmuring something in her ear before he came back. Gina's cheeks turned pink and Drake chuckled. It was a rare thing for Gina to blush. Caleb was good for her, and so was the babe in her belly.

And being surrounded by them was good for Drake. It was only when he was with those closest to him that he could relax his mental shields and let himself believe what he felt was real.

He had a lot more control over his shields now that he had Melissa in his life. When he was with her, they were on equal footing. No mystical, paranormal, or psychic powers that would let one know what the other was thinking or feeling. They had to talk, to communicate like ordinary people, and he loved it. He loved her.

He fingered the marquis-cut emerald ring in his jeans pocket and felt his gut clench. Deep down he knew she would say yes, but there was still that touch of uncertainty. And even that was wonderful, because he was actually feeling it.

"You gonna finally ask her tonight?"

Drake looked down at his side and grimaced at Nadya's smirk.

"You think I should?" he asked. "She's your sister. You've spent a lot of time together in the past year, almost more than she and I have since you spent all summer in Chadwick. Do you think she'll say yes?"

The seventeen-year-old woman looked him straight in the eye. "If she doesn't, I'll kick her ass. You two belong together."

Drake threw back his head and laughed loudly. Christ, life was good!

**THE PETSHANI:**
Shandor

A Bonus Short Story from Sasha White!

# 1

_____

I knelt reverently in front of the carved wooden box I'd pulled
from the corner of my closet. A tinge of shame echoed in my
heavy heart as I realized how long it had been since I'd laid
hands on the small chest. How long I'd been denying who,
what, I truly am.

My fingertips trembled as they traveled gingerly over the
carved symbols on the lid, and a shiver danced through my
body. Before any doubts could seep into my heart, I lifted the
lid of the box and reached for what I needed. Everything was
just as I'd left it. I began to remove the items from the chest one
by one. Soon I was sitting cross-legged in the middle of my
bedroom floor surrounded by four candles—a silver one, a
lavender one, a white one, and a pale blue one. The colors of the
Moon Deities.

My mother, my grandmother, my thoughts turned back into
the distant past. Memories of other magical women in my family pushed at my mind and I pushed back, not ready to deal
with them.

Directly in front of me lay the covered wooden box, now an

altar, with a plain silver goblet filled with white wine, an ebony-handled, silver-bladed athame that had been handed down through my family, and a quartz crystal. Jasmine incense wafted through the room, helping to ease me into a meditative state.

Ignoring the slight trembling in my stomach, I closed my eyes and concentrated. The moonstone pendant at my neck warmed and the power came easily, as if the time it had sat inside of me unused had only made it stronger, more eager to do my bidding. I knew this was an illusion, though. Power weakens when ignored; it doesn't rest and regenerate. As if to prove this fact, once I'd flicked my mind to the candles surrounding me and lit them, the energy flowing through my veins weakened to a slow pulse, drained.

Without opening my eyes, I reached for the crystal with my left hand. The quartz grew warm in my grasp and I felt the power of my ancestry surge through me, renewing, reminding me of all I'd ignored for so long.

I summoned the image from my dreams to my mind's eye, and braced myself.

He was tall, more than six feet, and solid. Dark hair swept back from rough-hewn features and bared dark eyes and full lips to my view. The lift of his head told me of his pride, his arrogance. But it did little to detract from the magnificence of him. His nakedness hid nothing from my view. My blood heated at the sight of his golden skin stretched taut over firm muscles. The glinting silver hoops that pierced his nipples shimmered in the air. There had to be some significance to them, but I didn't know exactly what it was, so I filed away the fact for future research.

I'd thought it was just my repressed libido manifesting him in my dreams. The fact that I awoke each morning for the last week from dreams of him wet between the thighs, but sated and heavy as only a well-fucked woman could be, should've warned me that there was more to him than being a simple dream lover. But it had taken him appearing to me in front of my desk at work earlier this afternoon—while I was wide-awake—to make me accept that fact.

Now, as I studied the image in my mind, preparing to call to Blodwin, Moon Goddess well versed in Lunar Mysteries and Dreams, a warm breeze drifted over me and a sense of magic filled the room. I slowly opened my eyes, only to have my breath catch in my throat. He was there. All six-feet-whatever of gleaming masculinity. In front of me. In my bedroom.

Sort of.

Trying not to appear as startled as I felt, I stood to face the translucent figure. Dressed in loose-fitting trousers, he was no longer naked, but close enough to make my heart race. A quick visual check showed me my circle remained intact.

"Who are you?"

He dropped to one knee and bowed his head. "I am Shandor Troika. At your service."

Well, his services had certainly been wonderful in my dreams, but . . .

"I think you have that backward, Shandor. It seems I'm at your service. Unless you plan to leave me alone after this little chat."

When he stayed on one knee with head bent, I realized he'd remain like that until I said otherwise.

"Stand up and face me."

He stood up straight, broad shoulders thrown back, muscled chest distractingly out. I dragged my gaze from those flat male nipples with the silver hoops that made my fingers itch to the swirling darkness of his eyes.

Once again my blood heated while my pulse raced and my body started to hum. The urge to strip and be touched made my head swim. What was happening?

"What are you?"

"I am Shandor, leader of the Petshani."

"I thought you were just a dream. I didn't think you were real . . . but you are. Obviously." I bit my lip to stop my babbling, and took another look at his see-through form. "Well sort of real, anyway."

"I am very real, Mistress, and in danger."

"Danger?"

"I've been trying to contact you." Shandor spoke in a firm, yet soothing voice. "My people—what's left of them—are in need of your help"

"My help? Your people?"

"Yes, Mistress." He stood, hands at his side, chin lifted and eyes straight ahead. Almost like a soldier. Yet, before now, he hadn't been afraid to meet my gaze.

"Please, Shandor. If you need my help, make me understand. Look me in the eye when talking to me, and speak freely."

His spine relaxed a bit, and he glanced at me with emotion-filled eyes. "We've declined to become exclusive to the King's House, and as a result, he has declared all Petshani criminal. We've been hunted, and now there are only four of us remaining. We have no family, no land. We need a new home, and only a blessed witch can open the portal to bring us through to your world so we can make one."

"You want me to find you a blessed witch?"

He looked steadily at me. "I've already found one."

Unease began to creep up my spine, only to disappear when I met his gaze and the hum of sexual arousal replaced it. I shook my head and tried to concentrate. "Okay, so you need me for what?"

"You, Mistress, are the blessed witch we seek."

Me? Blessed? My head spun, and the room tilted. "No way! First off, I'm not blessed; second, I'm not a witch anymore."

"There is no doubt. You, Mistress Karenna Logan, are the one we need." He glanced over his shoulder and his expression darkened. "I must go now. Please, Mistress, we need you to open the portal for us. You'll need this." He held out a flat silver disk.

Then he vanished.

My knees buckled and my butt hit the floor. The candles were still lit, the circle still complete. Yet he'd disappeared and the disk was shining in the candlelight two feet in front of me. What was happening?

I spent a moment trying desperately to make my brain focus on the reality of what had just happened. Reality? Ha! Maybe I was cracking up.

Time to call for a sanity check.

I closed my eyes and said a few words before putting out the candles with a wave of my hand. After crawling on the floor to the bedside table, I grabbed the phone and automatically dialed.

"Tessa?" I asked when a groggy voice answered.

"Renna! What's wrong, sis?"

"Something magically fucked up is going on—and I need your help."


Thirty minutes later a gorgeous redhead with lush curves and a lot of attitude strode without knocking into my basement suite—one of the disadvantages to living in a townhouse as opposed to an apartment: no security gate that visitors had to buzz to get into the building.

Contessa Logan placed a stuffed tote bag on my kitchen table and turned to me, her green eyes tinged with seriousness and her lips unsmiling. "Tell me."

"Some spirit ... ghost ... or something ..." I waved my hands in the air, trying to find the right word. "I don't even know what he was . . . just told me I was the only one who could save him and his people. That there were only four of them left and if I didn't help them, they would be killed. I'm supposed to open some portal and bring them through to this world! Why the hell is he coming to me when you're the witch in the family?"

She rolled her eyes before pinning me with a gimlet stare. "You're a witch, too. It doesn't matter that you chose to ignore the fact, it's still true."

"Whatever . . ." Confusion swamped me and I dismissed that part of the discussion. I'd given up magic years ago, until today.

"Fine," Tessa said. "Moving on, there are four of who? What was he? How does he say you're supposed to do this?"

"I don't know. He disappeared before we got to that part."

"Let me get this straight. Some guy just appears to you and says, 'Save me . . . save my people'?"

"He appeared in front of me at work today. Like a ghost, just standing in front of my desk." I shrugged. "When I got home, I cast a circle and was about to try for a vision, when he appeared in my bedroom."

Her face lit up. "You cast?"

I had known that would get her attention. "Yeah, something about him . . . I just had to figure out what was going on."

"That's great! You said you would never do magic again after what happened to Mom. Anyway . . ." She wisely changed the subject, a cocky grin spreading across her face. "What was he like? Was he super-sexy and seductive? Did you fall under his spell?"

I thought about it. "Actually, he was sorta militant."

Her face scrunched up in disappointment.

"When he was here, he stood like a soldier and kept calling

me 'Mistress.' But in my dreams he never—" I stopped myself and turned away. "Have you ever heard of others talking to people from another plane? Like an alternate universe or Otherworld?"

"Back up. What do you mean, 'in your dreams'? You've been dreaming about this guy before now and you never told me?"

"They were dreams! Erotic dreams of a hot sexy man. . . . I didn't think they were the types of thing I needed to share with my sister. I certainly didn't think they were some magical beings trying to communicate with me!"

"How do you know for sure he's not something evil trying to trick you? An incubus or sleep-stealer."

"I just do." I lifted my empty hands, palms upward, and shrugged. "It's strange, but I trust him." It was lame, but it was the best that I could do.

Tessa shook her head and smirked. Apparently lame was fine with her.

"The dreams were that good, huh? Damn! Why couldn't he haunt my dreams? At least I'd know what to do with him."

I glared at her. "Hey!"

"Sorry. It's just that those geeks you date hardly inspire passionate thoughts."

I bit my tongue. I felt like yelling at her not to judge. Tessa was flamboyant in everything, and her sexuality was no different. Sometimes she forgot that not everyone was as open as she was.

"In my dreams I never got a real close look at him. I mean, it was more . . . just a feeling, a presence . . . you know? And when he showed up at work, I just knew it was the man from the dreams. But again, he was ghostly. No one could see him but me . . . and let me tell you, when I summoned him here and

221

I got a good look at him, I also got to talk to him, and there's no doubt in my mind he's real. And he's in trouble."

My sister didn't go into shock or show any real signs of surprise at my words. Tessa just shrugged. "Mama always said there was an Otherworld, and travel between it and our world was possible for the right people."

Pain knifed through my chest at the mention of my mother. I missed her so much. When my heart stopped thumping in my ears, I focused on Tessa's words. A certain note in her voice made the hair on the back of my neck stand up.

I turned, as if to look outside, and watched her reflection in the mirror. "The right people? You mean like a blessed witch?"

Tessa's head dropped and she chewed her bottom lip.

Anger flared inside me. I spun around to confront her. "You knew! How could you know and not tell me? How come I've never heard of them, or not even know that I was one?"

"Renna, you walked away from our traditions after Mama died. You said you renounced our beliefs and refused to do magic. What was I supposed to do?"

"But how did you know when I didn't even know?"

"When you were a baby and wreaking havoc every time you waved your hands about the room, Mama knew you were special." She stepped forward and clasped my hands in hers. "She went away one day, and when she returned that afternoon, she said you'd been blessed. Mama said you weren't to be told until your twenty-first birthday and that she'd explain everything then. That's really all I know about it."

"Why didn't you tell me?"

"As I said, you renounced it all a year before you turned twenty-one. I figured if I left well enough alone, things would happen on their own. And they have."

"You know why I renounced it! This could've changed things. If I'd had a clue, I might've been able to help Mom!"

222

Tessa shook her head and looked at me with eyes full of love and compassion. "No one could've helped Mom. She didn't want help. She chose to sacrifice herself to protect us. We need to honor that choice."

My temper faded. "That doesn't make your not telling me right, you know?"

She straightened up and looked me in the eye. "I did what I believed was right."

I saw the hurt in her eyes and felt the love coming from her from three feet away. Steady and sure. A sigh escaped me. With an aching heart, I stepped forward and opened my arms to her.

"You're right. You did what was best. I was in no frame of mind to know this before." I hugged her tightly and welcomed her return squeeze before stepping back. "But now, what do I do?"

She pulled out a chair and sat at the table while I made tea.

"Who is this man that told you?" she asked.

After I explained everything that had happened over the past week, Tessa and I made plans for her to bring over Mama's journals the next day.

That night I lay in bed tossing and turning, trying to sleep, trying not to think about my mother and the past. I'd always loved being a witch. My mother was one, my older sister as well, and so was I. My father had died in a car accident before I turned five. Just before my twentieth birthday, my mom had died as well, leaving Tessa and I alone, all that was left of our family.

My mother had died while using her powers to heal. It wasn't a big dramatic war with an evildoer that had taken her from us. It was the fact that with power came responsibility. And she felt that, since she had been in the yard to witness a car hit a neighbor's child, it was her responsibility to use her power to heal the child's fatal internal injuries.

And it had taken all her power and life force to do so, leaving her so weak that I'd had to help her into the house, where she peacefully passed away on our sofa. She was glad she'd done what she'd done; she'd always said, "You have to help the ones you can . . . it's what is right."

What she hadn't known, however, was that I'd still needed her.

It was then that I'd sworn off the craft. My power scared me. I was stronger than both her and Tessa, and I hadn't learned to completely control it without them to balance me, to help me rein it. I hadn't been ready to let her go . . . and I still wasn't ready to accept that sort of responsibility.

Finally, when I slept, he came to me in my dreams. . . .

I was restless, tossing and turning in my bed, until I felt a heavy hand on my shoulder.

His hand.

I rolled over and saw him with one knee on my mattress, leaning over me with passion and excitement in his dark eyes. My heart kicked in my chest and my blood heated as he pulled aside my sheets and gazed on my naked form.

Light fingers skimmed over my body. First over the curve of my hip, the planes of my belly, then upward to firmly cup my breasts before running a fingertip around a rigid nipple. My back arched and I thrust my breasts forward, pleading for attention. Shandor's lips tilted and he lowered his body over mine. The feel of flesh against flesh, hard against soft, made me mewl with desire. His lips covered mine, hungry and urgent. His tongue thrust gently between my lips, delving deep into my mouth and claiming me as his.

There was no doubt I belonged to him. We fit together perfectly. His taste was the one for which I'd been waiting; his touch made my body come alive as it never had before. I wanted more—I couldn't get enough of those strong hands trailing heat everywhere.

His knee nudged between mine and I eagerly spread my legs. The hot steel of the erection that had pressed against my belly now brushed against my core.

"Please," I whispered in his ear.

"Yes, Mistress," he answered, his hot breath floating over my skin, a lock of his silky hair falling forward and teasing my cheek.

My hands cupped his firm butt, tugging urgently at him, pulling him closer, but not close enough. His cock slipped between my wet pussy lips only to stop at my entrance. He licked the side of my neck, nibbled at my earlobe, then pulled back to gaze into my eyes.

"If you save my people, I'll be forever in your debt and in your arms for as long as you want me."

With a firm thrust of his hips, he filled me, and I couldn't answer. His words needed a reply, but none would form. The only sounds escaping my lips as he pumped steadily into me were gasps and sighs of pleasure. He felt so good inside me. He filled me perfectly, and my body responded to every change in pace or angle as if he were a master musician and I his instrument.

The whole time that our bodies undulated against one another our eyes remained locked. With his swirling eyes full of promises of unlimited pleasures to come, his lips curled into a gentle smile. His hands cradled my head as he rested on his elbows, his chest brushing mine with every panting breath.

When my orgasm approached, I clutched his shoulders, my nails digging into the rippling muscles of his back. My insides tightened and I felt myself getting closer and closer to the edge.

I wrapped my legs around his hips and arched into him. My heart pounded and my pussy clenched as I fell over the edge into the abyss of pleasure promised in his gaze.

"Shandor!" His name flew from my lips as I jerked awake, tremors still racking my body. Unbelievable!

Cool air danced over my skin. I sat up to reach for the covers at the foot of the bed. Had I kicked them off?

Then I noticed the flat silver disk on my bedside table.

It was glowing.

# 2

Shandor Troika laid a firm hand against his pounding chest and opened his eyes.

Karenna was the one. He figured it was so when he'd found her in his dreams, and any doubts he'd had now vanished.

Her surprise at being told she was a blessed witch shocked him. How had she not known? Only those with the right blood were blessed. Only those that had the blood of a witch, as well as the blood of a true magical Gypsi, could be taken to the tribe's wise woman—the Shuvani—to be blessed.

Karenna was the one for whom he'd been searching, the one who could help him save his tribe. He closed his eyes again and reveled in the sexual satisfaction he'd received in pleasuring her.

As a Petshani, the tribe known to bring pleasure to those who could pay—be it by song, dance, conversation, or sexual loving—he didn't always receive enjoyment from pleasuring those who used his services.

But he had with her. Each and every time he'd slipped into her dreams, he'd achieved his own satisfaction. It had become addicting.

He'd promised her this night that if she helped him, he would be hers alone, and he'd meant it. She'd been strong enough to summon him with just her mind, and that night he'd seen in her eyes the truth of her soul.

No matter that they came from different worlds, he was meant to be hers.

# 3

"I found out who the Petshani are."

Tessa's head popped up and her eyes pinned me to the spot. She'd been sitting at my kitchen table again, her long red hair held back in a snug ponytail, her polished fingernails tapping impatiently on the tabletop as she leafed through various family journals. But now I had her full attention.

"Well?" she asked.

I tossed a couple of printed sheets on the table in front of her. I'd done some searching on the Internet and found a few references to the Gypsy Legend of Petshani.

After running some water, I put the kettle on to boil and tried not to stare at Tessa as she skimmed the pages.

"They're like Geishas!"

"Yeah, but not Asian. They're Romany. Some say they are a Gypsy legend, and we know that all legends are based in fact." My voice vibrated with excitement.

My sister gave me an appraising look. "You said you'd been dreaming about him?"

Heat spread over my cheeks and I glanced away. "Yeah."

A bark of laughter jumped from her lips. She smirked at me. "Must be some dreams. You're blushing so much, you're going to go up in flames in a minute."

"It seems like these Petshani are a special breed of Gypsy. They're warriors, poets, and entertainers. While all of them have every skill, they also develop their own specialty. It's how they survive."

"Specialties, eh?" Tessa suggestively wiggled her eyebrows.

A giggle escaped my lips before I sharply pursed them, and I gave her a mock glare. "They were prized for their gifts and abilities, with many people wanting them, but they were true to the Gypsy spirit and remained a nomadic tribe. They were— you know what? None of this matters. What matters is that one of them has found a way to reach out through time and space, so we need to help them."

Tessa gave a sharp nod and we went back to the journals. There had to be a spell or ritual in there that would help us free Shandor and the few people he had left.

"Renna! I think this is it." Tessa's head lifted from the ancient diary in front of her. "Not in Mama's notes, but in Grandmere's. Look."

As I read over the chicken-scratch writing in the leatherbound journal, my heart started to pound and adrenaline flowed through my veins.

I believed the ritual we found would succeed. I hadn't worked magic in a long time, and although cooking wasn't really my thing, I needed some herbs. But Tessa said she'd bring them over the following night. Saturday night. The moon was in its waxing phase and Tessa didn't have to work, so she could be there to help me. To anchor me.

I showered after Tessa left and wondered what the hell I was doing. Magic was something I'd shunned for a long time. It held too much responsibility. Just like this . . . how did I become responsible for saving this dream lover and his remaining people? And how was I going to do it?

I didn't kid myself. I couldn't walk away. I'd hidden from my fears and my mother's teachings for long enough. The universe worked in mysterious ways. This whole situation had happened for a reason and I had to trust that.

Somehow, I would discover how to open the portal in the right place and help my dream lover. It didn't matter that the ritual didn't exactly say what Otherworld it was for. In fact, I didn't even know how many there were.

What if I opened a portal to the wrong one?

My chest tightened as I toweled off, and I tried not to get worked up. Things would be okay. There was obviously something tying me to Shandor and I had to have faith that it would guide me to the right gateway.

I walked naked into my bedroom and thought about summoning Shandor again. Could I do it a second time?

After eyeing the caved wooden box sitting innocently against the wall, I crawled between the crisp sheets and tried to calm my heartbeat. Shandor had come to my dreams without my summoning him. And the night before, for the first time, he'd spoken.

If I could get the timing of the dream right, if I could be half asleep and half awake when he came to me, I might be able to control some of it.

Yes, Shandor would come to me again. I knew it.

And this time, I'd have some questions for him.

Hot breath floated over my skin a second before soft lips brushed mine.

I opened my eyes and smiled at the gorgeous man above me. "You came," I whispered.

"I'll always come to you when you think of me." A gentle

hand cupped my cheek, his thumb rubbing my bottom lip. "You are worried. I can feel it. What troubles you, my little witch?"

"My sister and I found a ritual to open a portal to an Otherworld, but I'm afraid. What if I open the wrong one?"

"You'll be fine. You are the one meant to do this. It's how I found you. I have faith in this." He pressed a kiss to my forehead. "I have faith in you."

His naked body pressed against the length of mine and I felt his cock stir against my thigh. Trying desperately to ignore the lust building inside me, I pulled back a bit.

"Shandor! How will I know to open it where you are? Do you know where the portal opens? Does it just open anywhere?" I pushed at his shoulders and sat up in bed. "I don't understand how this works."

"Shhh..." he whispered, sitting up behind me, his chest against my back. "You have a piece of me. Use it when you begin the ritual and I will know. When I feel you reaching for me, I'll reach for you, and the portal will open between us."

"A piece of you?"

He glanced pointedly at the silver disk on my bedside stand. It was glowing brightly again.

My brows drew together in a frown. "How is that silver disk a piece of you?"

"I put a charm on it when I forged it. As long as you have it, you can find me, no matter where I am." His firm hands wrapped around my waist, and he settled me on top of his lap. "No troubles. You are Mandi's Kam... mine to love, dear Karenna. I am meant to be yours, as you are meant to be mine. We will be together. Tomorrow. I've seen it."

He tangled long fingers in my hair, turned my head, and put his mouth to mine. Lust coiled low in my belly as we kissed, mouths opening, tongues searching, breaths blending.

232

Shandor filled my senses, his flavor slightly herbal, his scent a clean woodsy aroma. The strong muscles of his thighs flexed beneath me and I pressed against him. His hands gripped my hips, rocking me against him, the hard ridge of his erection sandwiched between our bodies. My pussy throbbed and my insides clenched hungrily. I planted my hands on his chest and pushed him back onto the bed.

When I pinned him, I trailed my lips over his neck, nipped at his ear, and tweaked his pierced nipples with my fingers. He was Petshani, used to pleasing others. For more than a week he'd been my dream lover and made each night unforgettable.

But this time I wanted so badly to please him.

I wiggled lower down his body, my mouth focusing on one ringed nipple while one of my hands circled his rigid shaft. So big. And hard. His hands roamed my back and buttocks. When I tugged at the silver nipple ring, he gave a moan of pleasure.

"Karenna, so good."

He didn't fight me or try to regain control. It was as if he instinctively knew that pleasing him would please me. I slid lower down his body and he bent one leg, insinuating it between my thighs so I could ride it when my lips touched his cock.

Here, a bit of musk mixed with his unique woodsy flavor. As I took him deep, I felt the throb of hot blood flowing through his thick, full erection, pulsing against my tongue. I cupped his balls and fondled them while I licked the length of his shaft. My lips formed a tight O over the shiny head, and I sucked it as my hand stroked his length. The need to breathe got stronger, and I went back to long, slow strokes. His hips lifted and fell with my rhythm, fucking my mouth.

His panting grew loud and his fingertips brushed against my ears. His balls tightened in my hand and his cock twitched against my tongue. In one fluid motion, his hands gripped my shoulders, lifting me away from him and throwing me onto my back.

His large, muscled body hovered over me, his hips slipping into the cradle of my thighs, and our mouths eating at each other.

"Yes, inside me! Now, Shandor!"

He flexed his hips and his cock thrust home, filling me and making the stars explode in my eyes. My inner walls clenched at him, milking him as he pumped fast and furiously, until a rough groan echoed in the room. He buried his head in my neck, his body trembling above mine, while his seed flooded my body.

I felt the soft press of a kiss on my forehead. The weight of his body faded from mine and I snuggled into the pillow, letting myself drift into a deeper sleep.

"Ready?" I asked.

Tessa's fiery curls bounced when she nodded from her standing position within the circle.

I closed my eyes and raised my hands, and power flooded my veins. Wind danced over my skin, and every fiber of my being felt electrified. Strong. Able to do anything. With Shandor's warm silver disk in my left hand, I placed my right hand flat against the wall. "With all that is in me, with all that I control, I open this door and reach for you."

I opened my eyes and saw the wall shimmer. Heat built beneath my palm. I fought the urge to snatch back my hand and shake off the burning sensation. It continued growing, heating to the point of pain.

"No, I want this door open! I command it to open!"

The wall gave way to a bright light so blinding that I stumbled back. The sound of clashing metals, curses, and fierce fighting filled my room.

"NO!" I put out my hand to stop Tessa from rushing forth, always eager to leap before she looked. "Wait until we can see."

When the light dimmed, my heart jumped in my throat. I saw Shandor on the other side in a grassy field with three others dressed similarly in leathers flanking him. The three, one of them obviously female, were fighting off attackers as Shandor faced the portal. When our eyes met, my body hummed, and everything in me wanted to reach out and pull him to me.

"We did it! Come through! Hurry!" I shouted.

Shandor shook his head and stepped back, drawing a lethal-looking curved sword from his belt. "Through the portal—go!" he commanded the others as he jumped into the fray.

More and more attackers chased after them. The portal remained open, but no one could come through while fighting.

"Tessa, use the shield spell." I might have more natural magical power than my sister, but she was older. Plus she'd never stopped using her magic or experimenting with new spells.

"I can't cast it over them. They're too far away!"

I tore my gaze from the battle in front of me. "Can you freeze the attackers or something?"

"No, but we can throw shocks from here." Her bright green eyes met mine and she grinned like a little kid. She stepped up beside me and readied herself. "Just like when we were kids, Renna. Only think bigger, and stronger."

"Okay," I said, trying not to think that I hadn't thrown out a shock since Tessa and I were teenagers playing pranks. "You start on the left, I'll start on the right. Now!"

I extended my right hand, my index finger pointed at the ugly guy attacking one of the Petshani. A small bolt of flame flew from my fingertip, hitting him on the side of the head. The bolt itself seemed weak, but my aim was true. His hair went up in flames. He stumbled backward, falling into the next attacker.

The Petshani looked over his shoulder in surprise and saw

us. Tessa and I worked fast. Soon, the attackers dwindled to a few. Two of the Petshani raced through the portal and landed on the floor in my room. Shandor and one man remained, still fighting.

"Shandor," I yelled. "Get your ass in here. We can hold them back, but we can't throw with you in the way!"

Shandor and the other Petshani turned and jumped through the portal. Tessa hurled firebolts fast and furiously while I stepped up, closed my eyes, and waved my hands over the portal. "We are done with your service. Blessed be."

After a sucking sound, the wall turned solid in front of me again.

I turned to see three men and one woman, almost naked but for leather pants, vests, and swords. Tanned flesh stretched over taut muscles that gleamed in the candlelit room. Their chests rose and fell with each panting breath as they looked around in curiosity.

The Petshani had the appearance of very primal beings. They were dangerous and seductive at the same time. Tessa gripped my forearm, her face a portrait of delight as she gazed at them.

Suddenly Shandor stood in front of me, his warm callused hands cupping my face, his lips planted on mine, real flesh-and-blood lips and tongue tasting and teasing. He pulled back slightly, his swirling dark eyes smiling down at me before he dropped to one knee, head bowed.

The other Petshani followed suit.

"Thank you, Mistress. We are in your debt."

Oh Lord! Shandor was mine . . . and I was his.

Turn the page
for a tantalizing sneak peek
at DRIVE ME WILD,
by P.J. Mellor!

Coming soon from Aphrodisia!

# 1

---

"No way in hell." Ryan Wright squinted in the late afternoon sun at his twin brother, Braedon, and wondered what kind of mess his sibling had gotten himself into this time.

"Please." Braedon cleared his throat, and took a draw from the sweating longneck before setting it back on the sun-bleached wood table between them. He glanced nervously around the deck of the deserted ice house before zeroing in on his brother again. "You loved the *twin trick* when we were kids."

"We're not kids now. We weren't kids the last few times, in fact."

"I wouldn't ask if I had any other choice. I'll never ask you for another thing. I swear."

"You swore last time." Ryan stood and threw some bills on the table, trying to ignore the way the hairs on the back of his neck stood on alert whenever he was near his twin brother. "Not only did it cost me several thousand, it damn near wrecked my life."

Braedon's hand on his arms halted Ryan's exit. "Please. Don't you think you're the very last person I'd ask for a favor?" He gave a bark of laughter. "Unfortunately, you're the only one I *can* ask. The only one who will do. What do you want me to do? Beg? I'll beg. Hell, I'll do whatever it takes to get you to help me, to agree to do this just one more time." He raked a hand through his short blond hair. "This is my life we're talking about here," he added in a strangled voice.

"My God, what kind of trouble are you in?" Ryan sank back into his chair and gauged his brother's expression. In his experience, Braedon's face told him more than his mouth. And right now it was telling Ryan his brother was scared shitless.

"I made some, uh, less then solid investments, took some chances that didn't quite pan out." He held up his hand. "I know, we all do that occasionally. But I thought I could fix it. I took out a loan. Then another. And another."

Dread clawed at Ryan's stomach. "I get the feeling these loans weren't from a bank."

Braedon scrubbed at his face and shook his head.

"How much?" Despite his firm resolution to not aid his irresponsible brother again, he reached into his open sport coat for his checkbook. When Braedon remained silent, Ryan looked up, pen poised.

"More than you can float me, this time," Braedon said in a choked voice.

"How much?" Ryan asked again.

"Eight hundred would get them off my back for a while."

"Only eight hundred dollars? Sorry, bro, but I don't understand how you can be so bent out of shape over eight hundred dollars."

"That's eight hundred *thousand* dollars . . . *bro.* And, like I said, it's only a payment."

Ryan stopped writing.

"I can't help you this time," he said, closing the checkbook and slipping it back into his coat.

"Ah, but that's where you're wrong, big brother. Like I said, you're the only one who can. And it won't cost you anything except a few days out of your life."

Ryan wrestled with the pros and cons. He'd told Braedon he was finished with him and his stupid get-rich-quick schemes and shell games, that he was tired of bailing him out every time he turned around. He paused, swallowing the dread. Then again, he did have some vacation time coming. He had no plans. And Braedon did look desperate. And he was his brother.

His shoulders slumped in defeat. "Okay, I'll do it. I'll pretend to be you. Just one more time." At Braedon's triumphant smile, he gripped his younger brother's shirt and drew him closer until their noses touched. Eye to eye, he said, "But I swear to God, this is the last time I'm bailing your sorry ass out. And there have to be some ground rules."

Braedon's blue eyes took on the cool turquoise Ryan had come to recognize as cocky arrogance. He tugged his wifebeater T-shirt from his brother's fists and stepped back with a satisfied smile. "Thanks. I knew you wouldn't let me down." His gaze scanned Ryan head to toe. "You'll need to lose the pretty-boy haircut. No one will believe my hair grew overnight."

"What about your job? I don't even know where you work these days."

"No problemo. I'm currently on permanent hiatus. I plan to find a better job, anyway." He dug in the pockets of his jeans. "Here's my license, and the keys to my car and my apartment. And my cell. Now give me yours. Then we'll switch clothes and shoes."

"Wait. You haven't heard my stipulations."

Braedon heaved a sigh and shifted his booted feet on the deck. "Go on."

"You will not contact anyone in my address book, either on the cell or my computer. I have some vacation time coming, so you don't have to worry about going into the office. You are not to touch or even look at my stock portfolio. I mean it. No selling or trading, no matter how great of a deal you think it is. And I expect you to treat my home and my belongings, including my clothes, with respect. Is that clear?"

"Man, I told you the fire was an accident."

"Is that clear? Because if it's not, I'm not doing this."

"Yeah, okay, it's clear."

"And one last thing."

Braedon arched his brow.

"Don't sleep with anyone I know this time."

"That wasn't my fault—"

"I don't care. Swear to me you won't sleep with anyone I know. Swear, or I call the whole thing off."

"I don't care if you sleep with anyone *I* know." Braedon held up his hands. "Okay, I swear. I swear." He looked across the parking lot at the highway. "Not that I'd be attracted to the skanks you date anyway."

Ryan took a deep breath in an effort to relieve the tenseness radiating into his shoulders. This was such a bad idea on all levels. But he'd do it. Just one more time.

# 2

---

Ryan watched his brother leave the parking lot with a squeal of the brand new tires he'd had installed on his Lexus SC430 the previous day, then glanced down at the keys in his hand.

A long time ago, he'd been an only child for a little over five blissful minutes. Then Braedon had put in his appearance, complaining all the way out of the womb, and had not stopped whining since.

Whenever he'd bailed Braedon out as kids, their grandmother always reminded him no good deed went unpunished. He thought of that as he walked to the back of the parking lot, not at all sure what he'd find, absently scratching along the neck of his brother's T-shirt.

What he saw made him blink.

A bright red Aston Martin Vantage convertible sat alone under the streetlight.

Just to be sure, he thumbed the keypad. The car elicited a blip, and the taillights blinked at him.

"No wonder he's drowning in debt," he murmured, sliding into the glove-soft leather driver's seat. He'd just read about the car in *Car and Driver* magazine. It ran an easy hundred and twenty-six thousand dollars. He ran his hand along the shift box, and caressed the leather covered steering wheel.

The motor purred so smoothly it almost gave him a hard-on.

Anxious to try out the *Sportshift* he'd read about, he lowered the top and took off after pushing the navigation system on Braedon's phone for home, and did his best to relax and enjoy the ride.

He grinned when the sexy computerized voice told him to take the next exit. Oh, yeah, he could definitely get used to driving a car like this.

Penny Harding sniffed and wiped her drippy nose. Braedon would be back. He always came back. She twisted the engagement ring on her finger, thinking about the fight they'd had, and wondered if his return would be a good or a bad thing.

Braedon Wright was gorgeous. She'd been thrilled when he'd sought her out at their company party. Breathless when he'd first kissed her. And positively orgasmic when he'd taken her, that first time, standing up against his sexy red car, along the side of the road by the beach.

In hindsight, she couldn't help but wonder if part of the earth-shattering orgasm wasn't due to the thrill of being with a bad boy, the possibility of being caught, literally, with their pants down beside a public road. The sex afterwards sure hadn't come close to that first mind-blowing time.

Her stomach hurt, just thinking about the hateful, awful things he'd said to her earlier. She walked to the fridge and pulled out a Coke, popping the top and chugging down half the can. Her burp practically rattled the glasses in the cherrywood cupboards. She looked guiltily around the abandoned apartment, then slowly walked to stare out the sidelight by the door. Where was he?

What had Braedon seen in her that no one else had ever seen? Had their last argument chased him away for good? Why was she so hesitant about setting a wedding date? Anyone in their right mind would beat feet to the altar. She knew he could certainly do better. Her blah brown hair and pale green eyes were nothing to write home about. Allergies prevented her from wearing much makeup. Not that she'd ever been any good at applying it, anyway. She glanced at her less than impressive chest. Maybe she should ask her father to pay for augmentations for her birthday.

Braedon had his flaws, but he was handsome and would make pretty babies. And in all probability, he was her last shot at marriage. Heck, to be honest, he was her only shot in her whole twenty-nine years. She would not blow it. When he came home—and he would come home eventually, he always did—she was going to be waiting for him. She would prove she wasn't pathetic and needy, prove her sexuality. The thought of Braedon having sex with anyone else tore at her, and she made a vow to be sexier, to be the aggressor, like he was always telling her to be. Who knew? Maybe she'd discover she liked being sexier, and it would push her into making that final step in her commitment to Braedon.

Ryan turned the car into the covered space with the apartment number above it and sat for a moment. He closed his eyes, listening to the distant sound of waves in the Gulf of Mexico breaking on the shore, and took a deep breath.

Braedon's apartment was just across a short expanse of grass. Ryan snorted. His brother had no respect for money. He'd left all the lights on.

It took a second to fit the key into the lock, but the tumblers eventually fell into place and the door swung open.

The first thing he noticed was a trail of yellow rose petals leading from the tiled foyer down a hardwood hallway. Tossing his keys on the small table by the door, he followed the petals.

Light flickered on the walls of the hall, causing him to wonder if there was a fire.

The door to the right stood open. He nudged it with his toe, his breath catching.

A goddess stood by the door on the other side of the room. Totally naked, her smooth skin glistened in the candlelight, burnishing her chin-length hair. She walked to him, a small smile on her glossed lips.

"Braedon," she purred, stopping just short of rubbing the tips of her tits against his skimpy shirt. "I was getting worried. It's not like you to be gone so long. Where have you been?" Her pale eyes widened. "I-I'm not quizzing you, honey. I was just worried." She stroked his erection, then slipped her hand into his jeans to hold him. "And horny." She smiled up at him. "You, too, I see." She reached for the top button of his fly. "Let's see if we can do something about that."

"Ah, I need a shower." Who the hell was she, and why was she in his brother's apartment? "I'm sweaty. Drove with the top down, then stopped and got a haircut, so I need to rinse off."

She frowned. "I thought you got a haircut yesterday."

*Shit.* "Yeah, well, I had to go back and have it redone."

"Are you okay?"

"Sure . . . why?"

She shrugged, causing him to force his gaze from her well oiled chest. "Your voice sounds odd. Like maybe you're coming down with something."

He coughed for effect. "Probably from the night air."

She nodded absently and he slipped into the bathroom, closing and locking the door. He dug in his pocket and pulled out Braedon's BlackBerry. "C'mon, pick up!"

When his own voice came on the line, he hung up and twisted on the shower controls, cursing his brother for forgetting such an important detail, like the woman standing naked on the other side of the door.

Rather than clear his mind, the steam of the shower wove around him, stroking his sudden erection, making him impossibly harder.

He jumped when the shower door opened and cool air surrounded him. Before he could find his voice, the woman stepped in. How had she gotten in?

"I locked the door!" *Smooth, Ryan, real smooth.* It was a safe bet that would not have been Braedon's first words.

She smiled and placed her cool hands on his chest. "Why'd you do that? You know that lock hasn't worked since you moved in." The steam activated the warm, sultry scent of her perfume to waft around him, making his mouth water. She took the soap in her hand and began lathering him. All over.

No working lock. *Great, Braedon, another thing you neglected to mention.*

He reached down to push her away and somehow ended up with his hands full of breasts. Slippery, warm breasts with pebbled nipples.

She stepped closer, evidently thinking he wanted to play. Given the circumstances, not a stretch of the imagination. Her tan hand, with short unpolished nails, dragged over and around his pectorals. Then that same hand stroked the quivering muscles of his abdomen, gliding lower to travel to the part leaping to attention. When she gently fisted his length, he closed his eyes, shuddering as he tried to dredge up thoughts of baseball.

Unfortunately, all he could see behind his lids was the woman in front of him with nothing on except umpire padding.

He groaned.

She must have taken that as a sign because she climbed on his body and took his mouth. Her kiss was teasing, innocent yet sexy. Before he realized what he was doing, his arms held her high against his chest, while his mouth devoured hers.

*Stop,* his mind screamed. *You don't even know her name. You're standing in a shower at your brother's house. The naked woman in your arms has probably fucked your brother in ways that are illegal in most states.*

She shifted position, breaking mouth contact to push down on his shoulders, bringing her breasts in line with his mouth, her warm, wet pussy branding his abs.

He'd stop. His tongue ringed a plump nipple before drawing it into his mouth. Soon. Just a few more seconds of luxuriating in the tactile pleasure surrounding him, in the smooth sexiness of the woman softly moaning in his arms. He would stop very soon. In a minute, at the most.

She bent to whisper in his ear, her boobs temporarily cutting off his air supply. Not That he minded. Her panting breath in his ear sent shivers down his spine.

"I'm so sorry, Brae, so very sorry," she whispered, nipping at his ear. He wasn't sure exactly how it happened, but her breast had once again insinuated itself into his mouth. Had that not happened, he was sure he would have stopped her.

"I hate it when we fight." She reached down and drew his hand up, guiding him until he stroked the smooth hairless skin between her legs. "Feel that? I had it done, just for you. It wasn't as unpleasant as I thought it would be. Maybe because I kept thinking about how much you would like it, imagining you licking me and kissing me *there*." She pushed his hand down farther. "Feel how much I want you, how much I need you." She shoved his fingers inside her wetness and gasped. "I don't know if I can wait until we get dried off."

The next few minutes passed in a sexual haze. Before he realized what either of them was doing, his dick was buried deep within her heat.

It liked it there.

Gasping for air, he waited for his muscles to stop vibrating. He'd never come so violently, so completely. And he could not do it again. He firmly set her on her feet, then turned off the shower, hoping she would take a hint.

His spine stiffened at the warm feel of female anatomy against his back. Evidently he'd have to hint harder.

Gently disengaging her roving hands from his chest, he stepped away and grabbed two towels from the heated rack just outside the glass door, and handed her one. The fact that the rack was heated—yet another frivolous way his brother spent his money—distracted him for a second. When he glanced back, she was gone.

Just as well. Maybe she went home. The thought should have been a good one, yet he couldn't help feeling a tad bereft. She could have at least said good-bye, great fuck or something.

He took his time refolding and hanging his towel, then strode into his brother's bedroom to see if he could find any decent underwear.

What he found took thoughts of underwear completely out of his mind.